BwB

ROOTS & FLOWERS

ROOTS & FLOWERS

FLOWERS

poets and poems on family

edited by

LIZ ROSENBERG

Henry Holt and Company ∾ New York

SPECIAL THANKS TO:

Joëlle Dujardin, editorial assistant extraordinaire; my husband, David, for many late-night and early-morning labors performed with patience and grace; Peter Cohen, who helped a lot; my son, Eli, who helped a little; Cheryl, who held the house together, dogs and all; each one of the poets; Jason Bell; Paula and Sonia Kessler; and my brother-under-the-skin and editor, Marc Aronson.

Thanks go to the many photographers who have captured important family moments and allowed their images to be used in this book. Permission for the use of the following photos is also gratefully acknowledged: Page 20, photo by Paul Burkard; page 62, photo of Marie Howe by Marion Roth; page 70, photo of Milton Kessler and his daughter, Paula, by Sonia Kessler; page 84, photo of Stanley Kunitz by Ted Rosenberg; page 142, photo of Naomi Shihab Nye and her son, Madison, by Jim Blaylock; page 166, photo of Liz Rosenberg and her mother, Lucille, by Ross Rosenberg; page 170, photo by Richard Frost; page 210, photo by Jacquelyn K. Atkins.

Henry Holt and Company, LLC
Publishers since 1866
115 West 18th Street
New York, New York 10011

Henry Holt is a registered trademark
of Henry Holt and Company, LLC

Library of Congress Cataloging-in-Publication Data
Roots and flowers: poets and poems on family / edited by Liz Rosenberg.
p.   cm.
Includes index.
1. Family—Juvenile poetry.   2. Children's poetry, American.   3. American poetry—20th century.
[1. Family life—Poetry.   2. American poetry—Collections.   3. Poets, American.]   I. Rosenberg, Liz.
PS595.F34 R66 2001   811'.54080355—dc21   00-59663

ISBN 0-8050-6433-8
First Edition—2001
Printed in the United States of America on acid-free paper. ∞
1   3   5   7   9   10   8   6   4   2

For my family,
all of it: past, present, and to come.

And for Milton Kessler and his.

CONTENTS

INTRODUCTION   3

MARVIN BELL   Statement   9
The Last Thing I Say   10
from *To an Adolescent Weeping Willow*   11

ROBERT BLY   Statement   13
For My Son Noah, Ten Years Old   15

DAVID BOSNICK   Statement   17
Home from Work   18

MICHAEL BURKARD   Statement   21
Entire Dilemma   22

DAVID CHIN   Statement   25
My Father's Note   26
The China Cupboard and the Coal Furnace   27

VICTORIA CLAUSI   Statement   35
A Letter to Mother   36

STEPHEN DOBYNS   Statement   39
No Map   41

MARIA MAZZIOTTI
GILLAN

Statement 43
Arturo 45
Letter to My Mother: Past Due 47
*My Son Tells Me Not to Wear My Poet's
    Clothes* 49
Heritage 50

EAMON GRENNAN

Statement 53
Taking My Son to School 55

DONALD HALL

Statement 59
My Son, My Executioner 60

MARIE HOWE

Statement 63
The Attic 64

ADRIENNE E.
IANNIELLO

Statement 67
Memory 68

MILTON KESSLER

Statement 71
Ballad for Dave 73
Plain Poplar 74
Secret Love 78

MAXINE KUMIN

Statement 81
*For My Great-Grandfather: A Message Long
    Overdue* 82

STANLEY KUNITZ

Statement 85
Journal for My Daughter 88
My Mother's Pears 95

GREG KUZMA

Statement 99
My Son Skating on Doane's Lake 101

RICH LANDERS   Statement   103
                           Genesis   104

SHARA McCALLUM   Statement   107
                           Wolves   108

MARGARET K. MENGES   Statement   111
                           For Angela   112
                           The Winter of Stories   113

JERRY MIRSKIN   Statement   117
                           My Father   118
                           Bronx Park East   119

GREG MOGLIA   Statement   123
                           On That Day   124
                           Pietro   125

KYOKO MORI   Statement   129
                           Seeing My Parents in New York   130
                           Uncles   132

MEGEEN MULHOLLAND   Statement   135
                           Our Father's Image   136

HOWARD NELSON   Statement   139
                           Weariness   140
                           In the Class for Giving Birth   141

NAOMI SHIHAB NYE   Statement   143
                           Wedding Cake   145
                           How Far Is It to the Land We Left?   147
                           Genetics   148

LINDA PASTAN

Statement 151
Notes from the Delivery Room 152
A Real Story 154

WILLIE PERDOMO

Statement 157
Unemployed Mami 159

KATHA POLLITT

Statement 163
Playground 164

LIZ ROSENBERG

Statement 167
White Slip 168
How Quickly, How Early 169

DAVID ST. JOHN

Statement 171
Hush 172

KATE SCHMITT

Statement 175
Leaving You 176

HENRY M. SEIDEN

Statement 179
Monty 180
Turtle Story 182

JASON SHINDER

Statement 185
Places He Wasn't 187
Because One Is Always Leaving 188

GARY SOTO

Statement 191
Worry at the End of the Month 192

BETTYE T. SPINNER

Statement 195
Her Story 196

GERALD STERN   Statement   199
     Waving Good-Bye   200

DEBORAH TALL   Statement   203
     Touched   204

PHILIP TERMAN   Statement   207
     *Instructions on Climbing Your Father's
     Garage*   208

ANTONIO VALLONE   Statement   211
     Peach Blossom Snow   213
     from *Learning to Dance*   215
     Camping Out in the Backyard   217

LI-SHEN YUN   Statement   221
     Saturday in Chinatown   222

BIOGRAPHICAL NOTES   225

SUGGESTED READING
AND LISTENING   235

INDEX OF FIRST LINES   243

ROOTS & FLOWERS

INTRODUCTION

In 1999 I assembled an anthology, *Light-Gathering Poems,* as a more cheerful sister to an earlier collection, called *Earth-Shattering Poems.* Similarly, this book, *Roots and Flowers,* is related to an anthology of poems for young people I edited a few years ago, titled *The Invisible Ladder.* Like that anthology, *Roots and Flowers* features photographs of and comments by the poets themselves. In both books, all the poets are living Americans. (The single exception is Milton Kessler who, tragically, died as the book was going to press.) There are highly prized, well-known writers side by side poets published for the first time in these pages. Also like *The Invisible Ladder,* this collection is geared to young readers but will, I hope, pass into the hands of poetry lovers of any age, as has *The Invisible Ladder.* The notion of this book as "kin" to another makes special sense because *Roots and Flowers* is all about kinship: about connection and disconnection, kind-ness and relatedness.

Why an entire anthology of poems, photos, and statements dedicated to family? I have found, teaching and traveling around the country, that all true poets, of every age, write about what is closest to their hearts. Naturally enough, this for many poets means family: mothers, fathers, sisters and brothers, cousins and grandparents, stepparents, uncles and aunts. Family is where we experience our first strong emotions; it is where we learn how to love and be loved.

Young people care deeply about their families, even when what happens in the family is not happy. "Home is the place where, . . . / They have to take you in," wrote the poet Robert Frost. Family is who we belong to, even when we feel we don't belong. It is a deep connection forged by shared history, memory, genetics. Children try hard to love the people to whom they are related by blood, adoption, or circumstance. It is fantastic, heroic, the effort they make! And it is no secret that these early relations set the stage for later dramas. Nor is it news to adults that the love we feel for our children, grandchildren, and other younger relations recaptures some of that fantastic, heroic passion of our youth.

The first poet in this book, Marvin Bell, notes in his comment on poetry and family: "Someday the son will look into a mirror and see there the face of his father or mother, and then he will know that when they said 'sweet dreams,' they meant it with all their heart. Poetry expresses what we mean with all our heart."

Poetry is also one of the places where we can learn about the larger world, things that we don't know along with the things we do. "Children should listen to poets; poets should listen to them!" the poet Gerald Stern advised us in *The Invisible Ladder*. It's hard for some adults to really remember their childhood, the actual experience of it. And it's hard for children to imagine what it might feel like to grow old, or to have children of their own. Poetry is, above all else, an act of empathetic imagination. When we read about being an adult, or living in faraway places, when we read about how we felt as children or how we feel as grandparents, we draw closer to a wider understanding of the world and all its inhabitants. This, it seems to me, is yet another kind of "kinship" hidden in this book.

I wanted to make an anthology of poems about "roots"—our parents and ancestors—and also about "flowers"—children and grandchildren, nieces and nephews. The flower need not be our own child or any blood relation at all: it may be a student, our son's first love, or a baby we hold for a few hours on an airplane, as Naomi Shihab Nye shows in her wonderful poem "Wedding Cake." It may be an as-yet-unborn child, or a child only imagined, a moment of celebration or of despair.

Milton Kessler's poem "Plain Poplar," for example, may seem at first to be overwhelming, furious, not a poem for young readers. His widow and his children thought long and hard about letting us publish it. But to me it is a very important poem in this book, because it makes us feel again the *power* of a parent's curse, the power of a child's curse. "Bad words" are not just some vulgar habit of the times; they are weapons and will be with us as long as we continue to use weapons against the people we love most. "Honor thy mother and father": parents and children know how terrible it is to disobey that injunction, regardless of religious background. We know we need to honor our roots and our flowers, because, finally, we are all connected in one enormous, living family tree. Poet Marvin Bell observes, "It's the family, or the absence of family, that shapes our deepest emotions." Family is where we first feel our connection to the rest of the world. It is also where we first feel our estrangement from it, our loneliness. One might say that family is the great, first experimental laboratory where we test out the possibilities of all human relations.

I have tried to represent a wide range of family bonds, from Maxine Kumin's great-grandfather to Jason Shinder's two young nieces. Our roots may be found in older siblings, ancestors, family gatherings, even in one's hometown, as we see in Michael Burkard's poem "Entire

Dilemma." There are teenage boys learning how to dance by practicing with their mothers, and others learning how to sneak home by way of their fathers' garage roofs. Poets write about mothers-to-be glowing like a room of full moons, and exhausted mothers feeding their children in the middle of the night, or the middle of a playground.

There is no single way to think of family, just as there is no single way to read a poem. There is no single way to experience family, no single way to experience poetry. Marie Howe writes in her comment, "We were eleven people living in one house—eleven stories—eleven times eleven." Not to mention all the listeners (or readers) of those stories.

Adrienne Ianiello, the youngest poet in this collection (she was twenty years old when she wrote "Memory"), comments: "Writing family poems feels personal, like sitting in my favorite chair. I know every detail of the story, I can feel every emotion, smell every familiar scent. . . . When they look at one of my poems, I would like readers to feel comfortable and want to answer back, to open up their photo album, to tell me their stories."

United States Poet Laureate Stanley Kunitz, at age ninety-five the eldest poet represented here, quotes the Russian writer Leo Tolstoy: " 'Happy families are all alike; every unhappy family is unhappy in its own way.' . . . That wild-eyed, bearded Russian, I sensed, was speaking directly to me, as great writers have a way of doing in their encounters; and he was telling me not to brood: my fate was mine to make."

Thanks to the lucky whims of the alphabet, *Roots and Flowers* begins with "The Last Thing I Say," a poem about a father learning to say the right thing to his thirteen-year-old son at bedtime. It ends with Li-Shen Yun's poem "Saturday in Chinatown," in which a granddaughter learns to keep silent in order to allow her grandmother to dream. Sometimes a family needs words, sometimes silence. Sometimes we are the elder, sometimes the younger. All of us are always changing, and poetry, that impractical art, gives some practical guidance in the art of fluidity.

The anthologist's secret grief is always the poem—or the poems—that got away. I wished I might have included poems by the great African-American poet Lucille Clifton, who writes so often and so beautifully about family, or the poem "My Mother's Lips" by C. K. Williams, in which he remembers his mother listening to him so intently that her lips moved along with his. There are many others. (See Suggested Reading and Listening, as well as the poets' biographies, for more suggestions.) One works within limitations of time, space, permissions editors, and budgets. (I always learn this late—to my sorrow and to my editor's dismay.)

My hope is that this book provides a good starting point for poetry. Also that it offers new ways to look at ourselves and at others; at our past, present, and future existing all together in this thing called family. It is said that in the Garden of Eden all parts of a fruit tree tasted sweet, not just the fruit but the roots, the branches, the bark, the twigs. Our human family tree is similarly filled with hidden sweetness. This book is a celebration of every tendril, leaf, and bud.

*Marvin Bell and his son
Jason, 1996.*

*Marvin with his wife, Dorothy, and sons,
Nathan and Jason, 1983.*

MARVIN BELL

It's the family, or the absence of family, that shapes our deepest emotions. My father came to the United States as a teenager from the country called Ukraine. Eventually, he had his own five-and-ten-cent store where I sometimes swept the floors. I felt a hole open up inside me when he passed away in my early twenties. But not long after that, I became a father myself. Then I knew what my father had felt when I was a boy. I remembered that he would tuck me in for the night, just as I have tucked in my own sons—first Nathan, and then Jason.

A father has to learn to close the door softly. A father wants to protect his children from the rougher parts of the world. A father has to learn to let his children grow up. Someday the son will look into a mirror and see there the face of his father or mother and then he will know that when they said "sweet dreams," they meant it with all their heart. Poetry expresses what we mean with all our heart. That is why poetry creates such strong feelings inside us.

THE LAST THING I SAY

to a thirteen-year-old sleeping,
tone of an angel, breath of a soft wing,
I say through an upright dark space
as I narrow it pulling the door
sleepily to let the words go surely into
the bedroom until I close them in
for good, a night watchman's-worth
of grace and a promise for morning
not so far from some God's first notion
that the world be an image by first light
so much better than pictures of hope
drawn by firelight in ashes,
so much clearer, too, a young person
wanting to be a man might draw one finger
along an edge of this world and it
would slice a mouth there
to speak blood and then should he put that wound
into the mouth of his face,
he will be kissed there and taste
the salt of his father as he lowers
himself from his son's high bedroom
in the heaven of his image of
a small part of himself and sweet dreams.

FROM TO AN ADOLESCENT WEEPING WILLOW

I don't know what you think you're doing,
sweeping the ground. You
do it so easily, backhanded, forehanded.
You hardly bend. Really, you sway.
What can it mean
when a thing is so easy?

I threw dirt on my father's floor.
Not dirt, but a chopped green
dirt which picked up dirt.

I pushed the push broom.
I oiled the wooden floor of the store.

*   *   *

So Willow, you come sweep my floor.
I have no store.
I have a yard. A big yard.

I have a song to weep.
I have a cry.

You who rose up from the dirt,
because I put you there
and like to walk my head in under
your earliest feathery branches—
what can it mean
when a thing is so easy?

It means you are a boy.

Robert Bly and his son Noah.

ROBERT
BLY

My children have always been very helpful and acute in their relations to my poems. If I gave a poetry reading in Minnesota an hour or two from home, I would take Noah with me; he was about eight then.

We were one day in a fifth- or sixth-grade classroom, and Noah had climbed under the desk where I was sitting. After a while he popped out and said, "Read the seal poem, Daddy." Then he popped back underneath. I did read it, and it turned out that he was right—it was a perfect moment to read that particular poem to the children.

When my daughter Mary got to be about eleven, I was editing a poetry magazine called *The Seventies,* and sometimes Mary would help me send back poems that I didn't want. She sat near me. I would pass the poems to her, tell her what she should say, and she'd write the note and send the poems back. That was in 1973. About two years ago a man came up to me after a reading in California, and said, "I have a rejection slip signed by your daughter." I said, "Really? What did she say?" The note goes this way:

> Dear Mr. Alfred,
>
> My father says to tell you that your poems don't have enough images in them. Don't pay any attention;

he says this to everyone. I think your poems are wonderful.

Signed,
MARY BLY

So I discovered that she was writing her own notes! She softened the
blow a little and gave her own opinion as well.

FOR MY SON NOAH, TEN YEARS OLD

Night and day arrive, and day after day goes by,
and what is old remains old, and what is young remains young, and
    grows old.
The lumber pile does not grow younger, nor the two-by-fours lose
    their darkness,
but the old tree goes on, the barn stands without help so many years;
the advocate of darkness and night is not lost.

The horse steps up, swings on one leg, turns its body,
the chicken flapping claws onto the roost, its wings whelping and
    walloping,
but what is primitive is not to be shot out into the night and the dark.
And slowly the kind man comes closer, loses his rage, sits down at
    table.

So I am proud only of those days that pass in undivided tenderness,
when you sit drawing, or making books, stapled, with messages to the
    world,
or coloring a man with fire coming out of his hair.
Or we sit at a table, with small tea carefully poured.
So we pass our time together, calm and delighted.

David Bosnick with his wife, Liz, and their son, Eli, 1994.

DAVID
BOSNICK

The first poems I remember were the ones they taught us in school, written by Robert Frost: "The Road Not Taken" and "Stopping by Woods on a Snowy Evening." One was like a sort of warning, and the other sounded like a Christmas carol.

But when I was about twelve, I went with my dad to a Yankees game. It was Old-timers' Day, and there was a poem in the front of the program in memory of Lou Gehrig. (He'd been gone a long time.) I only read it once, but the last verse is clear in my mind, like the first time I saw my son in the delivery room.

> Let this be a silent token,
> Of lasting friendship's gleam,
> A promise of faith unbroken
> Your pals on the Yankee team.

That one word, *pals,* just killed me. My throat got tight, and my eyes began to sting. I felt silly. I glanced up at my father, the longshoreman, a hard guy from the Bronx. A dozen years from the war that shaped him. He was reading over my shoulder, and his eyes were wet. "He was a good guy, I guess," Dad said. Then he looked out over the field with our cheap binoculars.

I've been writing poems ever since.

HOME FROM WORK

Here on the table, in an envelope
I thought was a bill, is a lock
of our baby son's hair my wife
has just clipped. It feels like down.

They are napping together, his face still
against her arm, and in the
late afternoon light, that holds them in
a warm yellow gold of spring
a dozen things that had followed me, fretting
and scolding home from work, evaporate
lose all weight, become details.

I'll hold still listening
to hear them stir and rise.

Michael Burkard and his sister Betsy in the backyard, circa 1952.

MICHAEL
BURKARD

I am from Rome, New York, and I first started writing "poems" in my junior year of high school. I had enjoyed my family, but looking back it seems we stopped talking as we were growing up, and I needed to talk. Or I needed to talk about my troubles, whether I talked directly/openly or in a hidden/secret way. I have a book entitled *My Secret Boat* (W. W. Norton, 1990) that speaks to some of this.

ENTIRE DILEMMA

I wish you had knocked on my door today,
because I've realized I've had the entire dilemma
upside down. It will not seem important to you,
but you see, it has not been my parents who have
made me lonely, deeply deeply cold, over many

years and bridges, it was never them at all.
All this time I thought so, but I've had the entire dilemma
upside down. It will not seem important to you,
which is why you did not knock, but it has been the town
I was born in, town my parents remained in, town I returned

to like a dead bird still flying in search of a dead bell,
a soundless one the town likes to ring coldly out into the sky
at five o'clock or six o'clock or whenever one of the important
persons wants someone less important to know they are counting
money so they ring the bell—it is the town which has made

me sick all these, a town! And it made my parents sick,
and it made my brothers sick, and it made my sisters sick,
perhaps my sisters sickest of all—for they were always the ones
who were told you have nothing to be sick about, stick around
and see. They saw! Their poor eyes hardened like coins on a shelf,

and my relatives walked into our house to count these coins,
and slowly but surely they took my sisters apart, my little sisters!
And my brothers and I have returned and returned—because my

father was there, because my mother was there, and she is still
and is now very sick indeed and old, and yet never knew

we had the entire dilemma upside down. It will not seem important
to you, but you see it has been the town all these years.
It was not the roads we loved, it was not the houses,
—we actually hated the houses but we could not tell,
we hated the roads there but we walked upon them like ghosts

of deep habit, searching for passports, illegal passports, which
would place us in another country where someone is important
for you, knocks at your door, and whispers get out, get out,
long before you have heard the rivers in the words, the words
which come close, only to stray, only to judge you like the person

you are not, like the person on the top of a bell, being told
now, now, come down, come down from your bell you little dead bird.
It is five or six o'clock. The blackbird is sewing a song for you
to wear. A heavy song. All the heavier, for it is a song you will
always wear, and wear it upside down.

It has been the town I was born in.
It has made me sick. It has killed people, over and over.
Everyone tells everyone you are nothing in my town, and it is meant.
I wish you had knocked on my door today,
because I've realized I've had the entire dilemma upside down.

David Chin (on his mother's lap) with his mother, father, and sister.

DAVID
CHIN

Where did I come from? What makes me, me? Where am I going? Who can I become? We look for answers to these questions and discover wise old sayings: "As the twig is bent, so is the tree inclined," and "The apple never falls far from the tree."

When we want a reassuring connection to our past, we hope these wise old sayings are true. On the other hand, when we want to feel in charge of our own growth, or decide for ourselves how far we will travel, we hope these wise old sayings are not true.

Our sense of self and the way we relate to others have their roots in our connection to our families. Every family has its own small, but powerful, collective memory. Sometimes our family's memory is sad; sometimes hilarious. This memory may have its roots in secret wounds and nearly unspeakable pain, or this memory may have its roots in love, everyday sacrifices, and deep gratitude. Most often it is a mix of both good and bad.

I write about my roots—my childhood, parents, and family—in order to feel and stay close to my memories. Sometimes I write to look for a new way to understand a bad memory. Sometimes I write to celebrate a good memory. Sometimes I mix good and bad together and change them all around to make something completely new and different—then I feel like an unbent twig and a faraway apple!

MY FATHER'S NOTE

After the oral surgeon
pulled all of my father's
remaining teeth in one day,
my father sat stock still

in a rocking chair
all afternoon and half the night.
My mother sat with him.
The next morning he went back to work.

On the small table
between their chairs,
the little piece of paper
with his penciled messages to her:

—*it hurts*
—*terrible*
—*thirsty*
—*thank-you*
—*I love you*

A half dozen teeth yanked
and his silent jaw wounded
down to the truth telling bone.

THE CHINA CUPBOARD
AND THE COAL FURNACE

1

Laurel and Hardy wrestle the china cupboard
up the steps, but I don't laugh; their eyes
are tired with wine, their breath stinks of wine.
Stanley says, "Move over, kid, we don't need any help."
Mom signs the paper. They climb back into
the red Salvation Army truck.
A low hanging branch drops to the street.

2

At six o'clock Dad will bring home groceries.
A porterhouse steak to fry with garlic and ginger
then mix with broccoli or sometimes snow peas.
The rice will cook in the big pot
and when he lifts the cover, clouds of white steam
float up, like rabbits from a magician's hat.

3

Inside, she rips Dad's flannel shirt in half,
then nervously opens a bottle of furniture polish.
I stare at the carving on the two big doors
and think of Pastor Drummond behind the pulpit,

his white hands gripping its edges as he speaks.
He is talking about Adam and Eve.
Given a rag, I go over the dark-grained wood
discovering each dent and scratch.

4

"Why do you always bring this junk—"
"If I waited for you—"
"You don't care what the neighbors think."
"I don't. It's here. It stays."

In black and white, Rin Tin Tin
protects the Indian half-breed from bloodthirsty
ranchers—it's all a big misunderstanding
that started when the ice bridge melted
and the Bering Sea was born.

Rin Tin Tin saves the day.
Corky in a crew cut chortles.
Things return to normal back at the fort.

The credits roll, but the idea of the red
Salvation Army truck parked in front of our house
has made my father furious. Dinner is delayed.

Dumb dog, stupid happy ending.

5

The house pulls to a familiar tension—
the *Mayflower* cannonading the *Empress of Asia.*
The first floor stretches tight to cover
the cellar's unfinished earth. I go down there
where it's dark to consider the myth of my father's failure.
The coal furnace is an octopus with robot arms
holding up the house. If I put my ear
to the warm sheet metal, I hear the argument.

6

The furnace door opens like a bank vault.
The red glow throws my shadow
across the bone-dry ceiling joists,
across the mortar emptied crevices of the stone foundation.
It sharpens the points on exposed nails—
the first floor's underside—and draws the gray cobwebs
to the black shadows of copper water lines.
I throw a piece of coal the size of my fist
into the blaze and close the furnace door.

7

I helped put those copper water lines in.
I held the Benzomatic torch as he rolled
the flux dipped pipe in the brilliant blue flame
and made the elbow joints—the twisted, tortured
bends and turns that clatter and sing

when the faucets find the right radio station.
She had to tell him to let me help.
I tune in chalksqueak on blackboard a lot
just to aggravate them.

8

Superman could do it.
Superman could make us billionaires.
He can make diamonds from coal just by
clenching his fist. The coal bin's two ton heap
gleams blue and black. The bench vise just makes black dust.
I consider digging a tunnel with the coal shovel—
it's two blocks to the Trust Company of New Jersey.
I trace a floor plan in the dirt with a screwdriver
but give up—not enough shoring timber
in the crawl space under the kitchen.
On the Bizzaro planet diamonds are worthless.

9

Upstairs the polished shelves of the china cupboard
will soon begin adding up the years—
mismatched plates, birth certificates,
wedding invitations, locks of baby hair,
pale orange report cards, a teacher's
fountain pen cursive praising my deportment,
a souvenir platter from Niagara Falls,
Dad's lost, regained citizenship papers,

his jar of poker change, race track binoculars,
the removable plug to the TV Mom hides
in an unused rose decaled sugar bowl,
Mom's bible, a Chinese-English dictionary,
Dad's machine shop calipers,
and the ceramic ballerinas my sister made:
pink for pepper, blue for salt,
the blue one with its broken arm glued back on—
a triumph of bric a brac over mild empathic failure.

10

Dad banks the fire at bedtime
and shovels coal at six A.M.
If I'm the first one down, I stand
on the dining room register closest to the furnace
with my blanket draped from my shoulders to the floor.
I wait to catch the first bit of his warmth.
The scrape of his shovel in coal ash and cinders,
the rattle and grind of the grate
float up as if from the center of the earth.
Mom's already making pancakes.
When my sister wakes, we share the blanket.

11

I could live in this attic—
a castle turret I retreat to after school,
a window under the eaves of the roof,

under the point of a triangle.
I look down on the front doors
of the houses leaning into one another
up and down this street
and try to imagine the forest before
and the Revolutionary War
or think about the telephone wires,
dark against the sky, criss-crossing,
connecting everyone with everyone else.
And the pigeons and sparrows perched
on the TV antennas and the rooftops,
alleyways and the steady flow of cars
down this sidestreet. Intersections
adding up, asphalt connecting everything.
It's dry and dusty up here.
The window is covered with dirt,
but it's higher up,
the highest part of the house.
I'll have to come down.

Victoria Clausi holding her grandson Johnathon.

VICTORIA CLAUSI

The editor of this anthology asked if I might send her a photo of my mother and myself, or one of my mother and my aunt, even, to include with my poem. The truth is, I don't have any photos of my mother or my aunt, and none of myself before the age of eight, when I went to live with my mother. That truth says much about the "roots" of this poem.

Often poets are concerned with developing a sense of rootedness or place in their poems. Hometowns, ancestral farms, even family members are subjects frequently used to express this quality. But sometimes poets feel little or no connection to specific physical places or groups of people, so rootedness must be invented within the poet's heart and mind. Sometimes poets need to speak of change as rootedness. Sometimes the poet's work itself becomes the "place" of rootedness.

A LETTER TO MOTHER

Dear Jessie:

I'm worried about the world.

I inherit my worry from my schizophrenic mother
who once told my brother that she prayed all day
for her children—and that at night
she prayed for the rest of the world.

Tell me what you see, Mother,

I planted roses this year—in the southwest corner—
two old-fashioneds, a Graham Thomas and a Heritage;
two hybrid teas, a John F. Kennedy and a Peace:
cream, pink, ivory, yellow with peach edges
like erudite minds blushing toward sanity.

Tell me what to do.

Yesterday, a storm beat the Graham Thomas;
unruly canes arced toward the ground;
five-leaf stems broke; and everywhere petals,
bruised by rain, folded in on one another
or lay upturned on the pine-needle mulch.

What's my purpose in this world?

The Heritage is fighting a fungus
I fumigate weekly with clouds and clouds—
fog the tops, the undersides,
all the leaves—before blackspot covers
the whole plant, the whole garden.

And Aunt Stella called from Riverhead today, stuttering.
Something about the meds not being quite right:
Zoloft, Prozac, Nardil, Elavil, Wellbutrin.
"Or m-maybe I'll try Shock—it's n-n-not as bad as it used to be.
Some short-term m-m-memory loss."

"Doesn't that come back sometimes?"

"I d-d-d-don't know. But maybe it wouldn't
be so b-b-bad if it d-d-d-didn't."

Tell me what you see, Mother—

Maybe my raised bed doesn't get enough light?
six hours, tops, on the sunniest days. I think
roses need full sun, from morning till night,
and it has been storming for 28 straight days.

what wild blue iris opening?

Stephen Dobyns and his son.

STEPHEN
DOBYNS

When my son Emery was born, along with great joy I experienced an anxiety I had never known before. It was like being tossed three precious glass balls at once and not knowing if I could catch them. A friend explained this feeling by saying I had become "a hostage to the future," a phrase that was new to me. But I realized that at thirty-nine, I had never known fear and now I felt fearful. Not for myself but for my son. How could I protect him? I mean, protect him all the time? It was dangerous out there, and he was soft and sweet. And I knew my weaknesses. I couldn't just turn my life over to him. I had my work, my art, my other commitments—he would only have part of my time. Perhaps a large part, but only part. And when my back was turned, who knew what might happen?

The irony was that the more I loved him, the more I worried. It made me think of the poets Yeats and Rilke, who had said that one must choose between life and art—that one couldn't have both. And while Whitman and Neruda—other poets I love—took a contrary position, they didn't raise children (Neruda had a retarded daughter who was institutionalized, which must have been awful for him). Yet I had wanted this son; I had desperately wanted him, though my life eventually tugged me in other complicated and painful directions. And so the poem "No Map"—and others on similar themes—

rose up out of a combination of gut and heart. How do you protect those you love? You can only protect them a little bit as you watch them make their precarious way through a world both glorious and treacherous.

NO MAP

How close the clouds press this October first
and the rain—a gray scarf across the sky.
In separate hospitals my father and a dear friend
lie waiting for their respective operations,
hours on a table as surgeons crack their chests.
They were so brave when I talked to them last
as they spoke of the good times we would share
in the future. To neither did I say how much
I loved them, nor express the extent of my fear.
Their bodies are delicate glass boxes
at which the world begins to fling its stones.
Is this the day their long cry will be released?
How can I live in this place without them?
But today is also my son's birthday.
He is eight and beginning his difficult march.
To him the sky is welcoming, the road straight.
Far from my house he will open his presents—
a book, a Swiss Army knife, some music. Where
is his manual of instructions? Where is his map
showing the dark places and how to escape them?

*Maria Mazziotti Gillan with
her daughter, Jennifer. Maria is
holding a picture of her mother
and herself as a child.*

*Maria Mazziotti Gillan with her son,
John Gillan, four months old.*

Maria Mazziotti Gillan

In grammar school I remember Mrs. Ferraro standing in front of the room in her conservative dress, reading to us from a book, poems by Longfellow and Wordsworth and Edgar Allan Poe and Coleridge and Tennyson. Her voice reading those poems taught me the magic and music of language read aloud, as no one ever read aloud to me in my home where English was not spoken. To hear those poems read in the battered classrooms of P.S. 18 in Paterson, New Jersey, lifted me into another place and time as nothing else ever could. I loved the delicate and powerful way Mrs. Ferraro carried the words of the poems in her mouth, and I never forgot her or the power of poetry to move me to love and praise.

For years, when I wrote poetry, I tried very hard to be Keats or Shelley, to write in the English literary tradition I had been taught to admire. I was forty years old before I realized that I had to stop pretending in my poems, that I had to learn to write about the truth and beauty of Nineteenth Street in Paterson and of my life and family. The poet William Carlos Williams said, "The universal is in the particular," and I finally understood that if I wrote about my American life, my working-class, Italian-American life, the poems would form a bridge between my life and the lives of others. Poetry then became a way for me to save the people I loved, to pass them on to my children and to the children of others. I think we all have stories to tell about our lives, and we simply have to give ourselves permission to tell our stories in our poems.

Poetry is, for me, rooted in the body and in the earth. It is plain and simple and direct and specific. It has to be willing to take risks, to go forth into the world without masks or lies.

ARTURO

I told everyone
your name was Arthur,
tried to turn you
into the imaginary father
in the three-piece suit
that I wanted instead of my own.
I changed my name to Marie,
hoping no one would notice
my face with its dark Italian eyes.

Arturo, I send you this message
from my younger self, that fool
who needed to deny
the words
(Wop! Guinea! Greaseball!)
slung like curved spears,
the anguish of sandwiches
made from spinach and oil;
the roasted peppers on homemade bread,
the rice pies of Easter.

Today, I watch you,
clean as a cherub,
your ruddy face shining,
closed by your growing deafness

in a world where my words
cannot touch you.
At eighty, you still worship
Roosevelt and J.F.K.,
read the newspaper carefully,
know with a quick shrewdness
the details of revolutions and dictators,
the cause and effect of all wars,
no matter how small.
Only your legs betray you
as you limp from pillar to pillar,
yet your convictions remain
as strong now as they were at twenty.
For the children, you carry chocolates
wrapped in gold foil
and find for them always
your crooked grin and a five-dollar bill.

I smile when I think of you.
Listen, America,
this is my father, Arturo,
and I am his daughter, Maria.
Do not call me Marie.

LETTER TO MY MOTHER: PAST DUE

Today you tell me your mother appears
to you in dreams, but she is always
angry. "You're wrong," she screams.
You see her as a sign;
when she visits your nights, a cloud
of catastrophe bursts on your house.

Ma, hearing you tell me about her,
I see you, for a moment, as a young
girl, caught in a mahogany frame,
a young girl in a thirties wedding
dress with a crown of flowers in your
hair, your eyes deep and terrified,

see you leaning on the rail of that phantom
ship, waving one last goodbye, think
of you, writing to her, year after year,
sending her stilted photographs of your
children, a photo of yourself, your body
young and firm in a flowered dress.

You never saw her again.
She comes to you now only in dreams, angry she
comes. Did she, once, show her love as you
do, scolding, always scolding, yet always
there for me as no one else has ever been?

Once, twenty years ago, a young man bought
my dinner (oysters and wine and waiters
with white cloths draped over their arms),
forced his way into my room in that seedy
Baltimore hotel, insisted he would teach me
how to love, and as I struggled, you called,
asked, "What's wrong? I know something's
wrong." I didn't understand how you could
have known.

Yet even now, you train your heart on us like radar,
sensing our pain before we know it ourselves
as I train my heart on my children.

Promise me, Ma, promise to come to me in dreams,
even scolding, to come to me though I have been angry
with you too often, though I have asked you
to leave me alone. Come to me in dreams,
knowing I loved you
always, even when I hurled my rage in your face.

MY SON TELLS ME NOT TO WEAR
MY POET'S CLOTHES

My son tells me not to wear my poet's clothes. "They're weird," he says. He wants me to look like an old-fashioned grandmother, someone out of an L. L. Bean catalog, in a preppy sweater and a corduroy skirt, the kind of clothes that would have been all wrong for me even when I was 20 years old and 104 pounds. I love thin flowery dresses that float around me when I walk, long colorful scarves with fringe on them. My son does not say it out loud, but I know he thinks I'm the wrong kind of mother and that I should act my age and give up my poetry because it is strange for me to be running off to all those poetry readings and giving workshops and working so many hours a week at my job. Sometimes I think we should trade places. He could be the staid, conservative mother and I the recalcitrant son. When we talk on the phone, I hear how he shoulders the responsibilities of his life: wife, children, job, house, yard. "John," I say, "you're only 31. Give yourself a break." I hear him sigh, that expelled breath fraught with meaning that is the sound I make when I am anxious or bored, and I am saddened when I hear it coming from him over the wires across all that distance, not only the landscape that separates us but the language that fails us. I cannot find a way to make him understand that I love him, this son who needs to be far away from me so that it's as though I am chasing him down a path but he's always faster than me. I see him sitting with his son Jackson in his arms, Jackson who looks just like John did at two, and I see the way they lean together, Jackson so relaxed and trusting, his ear pressed to his father's heart.

HERITAGE

I'm like those Russian peasant dolls
made of lacquered wood where the larger dolls open
to reveal smaller dolls, until finally
the smallest doll of all stands, unseamed and solid.

When you open me up: my mother, her mother,
my daughter, my son's daughter. It could go on forever,
the way I carry them inside me.
Only their voices emerge, and when
I speak to my daughter,
I hear their words tangled in my own.

Ma, when you died, I thought I'd lost you forever;
grief washes over me
when I pass your barren garden and remember
the tomatoes that grew so wildly while you
watched from the bedroom where you were dying;
or when I walk into your basement kitchen
and see that it is grimy with neglect;
or when I see Dad sitting in the big recliner,
his legs covered by a blanket you crocheted
and a picture of you propped up
on the table next to him,
but when I open myself
you are still there inside me and I am safe,

even though I cannot drive to your house
or sit down while you pour me an espresso.
This is the way it is with me—
you are nested inside me,
your voice a whisper that grows clearer
with each day.

Eamon Grennan and his son, Connor, at Connor's college graduation.

EAMON
GRENNAN

I remember my older daughter, Kate, once saying to me—she must have been about twelve or so at the time—that the poems I'd written about her and her brother, Connor, seemed all to take place at a moment when they were leaving me or I was leaving them. It was true. What I wrote about them mostly took place at some instant when I felt a gap—the gap that has to be there between you and your children anyway—widening between us. Or else the poem sprang from an incident that (as I saw it) stood for a time in their lives that marked some decisive change or another, some setting-off into the world in a new way.

So I've written poems about saying good-bye to my son at the train station when he was going to live with his mother, or when he was taking his first bus ride alone; for Kate I've written of a moment when she goes out into the world alone as a six- or seven-year-old (waiting for the school bus), or about when she and I gathered mussels together and she was, I could see, turning from a girl to a young woman. I've written about my youngest daughter, Kira, in a slightly different way, but there is also often in these poems, too, some sense of farewell, of watching something that I know is terribly fleeting.

And I guess that's where the link between childhood and poetry comes for me. For poetry is always a sort of elegy. Even in celebration and even in love poems, there's always a sense that what I'm recording is passing away and that what I'm doing is trying to hold on to it, to hold it up to the light, in some sense to stay it, not let it go. Of course it goes, and that's wound into the poem, too, tuning the whole thing. Built into childhood, I suppose, is the myth of departure and loss (which is at root the sense of mortality itself deep inside us). But that root, or so we hope, produces a flower or two. The poems, that is, say, "Look, this happened!" Or they say, "This was so!" And being so, even *having been so,* is a blessing.

TAKING MY SON TO SCHOOL

His first day. Waiting, he plays
By himself in the garden.
I take a photo he clowns for,
Catching him, as it were, in flight.

All the way there in the car he chatters
And sings, giving me directions.
There are no maps for this journey:
It is the wilderness we enter.

Around their tall bespectacled teacher,
A gaggle of young ones in summer colours.
Silent, he stands on their border,
Clutching a bunch of purple dahlias,

Shyly he offers them up to her.
Distracted she holds them upside down.
He teeters on the rim of the circle,
Head drooping, a flower after rain.

I kiss him goodbye and leave him:
Stiff, he won't meet my eye.
I drive by him but he doesn't wave.
In my mind I rush to his rescue.

The distance bleeding between us,
I steal a last look back:
From a thicket of blondes, brunettes,
His red hair blazes.

It is done. I have handed him over.
I remember him wildly dancing
Naked and shining, shining
In the empty garden.

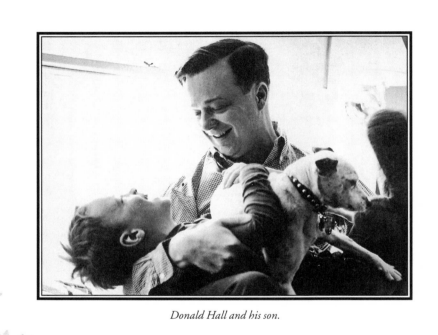

Donald Hall and his son.

DONALD
HALL

The ecstatic and contorted love of parent and child overwhelms us, in the time when we are children, through the time when we have children, through the time when we have children and grandchildren and become the dying generation.

MY SON, MY EXECUTIONER

My son, my executioner,
 I take you in my arms,
Quiet and small and just astir,
 And whom my body warms.

Sweet death, small son, our instrument
 Of immortality,
Your cries and hungers document
 Our bodily decay.

We twenty-five and twenty-two,
 Who seemed to live forever,
Observe enduring life in you
 And start to die together.

Marie Howe.

Marie Howe and her brother John in the 1970s.

MARIE
HOWE

We were eleven people living in one house—eleven stories—eleven times eleven. Over time: eleven times one thousand. In the fullness of time perhaps there is no "what happened"—what persists is the song. What endures? Gratitude, love.

THE ATTIC

Praise to my older brother, the seventeen-year-old boy, who lived
in the attic with me an exiled prince grown hard in his confinement,

bitter, bent to his evening task building the imaginary building
on the drawing board they'd given him in school. His tools gleam

under the desk lamp. He is as hard as the pencil he holds,
drawing the line straight along the ruler.

Tower prince, young king, praise to the boy
who has willed his blood to cool and his heart to slow. He's building

a structure with so many doors it's finally quiet,
so that when our father climbs heavily up the attic stairs, he doesn't

at first hear him pass down the narrow hall. My brother is rebuilding
the foundation. He lifts the clear plastic of one page

to look more closely at the plumbing,
—he barely hears the springs of my bed when my father sits down—

he's imagining where the boiler might go, because
where it is now isn't working. Not until I've slammed the door behind

the man stumbling down the stairs again
does my brother look up from where he's working. I know it hurts him

to rise, to knock on my door and come in. And when he draws his
  skinny arm
around my shaking shoulders,

I don't know if he knows he's building a world where I can one day
love a man—he sits there without saying anything.

Praise him.
I know he can hardly bear to touch me.

Adrienne E. Ianniello and her brother Jeff.

ADRIENNE E. IANNIELLO

I have been writing poems about my family since I first began writing at age fourteen. I love to create a poem that, like a photograph, can reveal a single part of my family: one face, one glance, one feeling, one memory. These poems are very important to me because all together they form my life's most vivid photo album, to which I can return often and remember.

Writing family poems feels personal, like sitting in my favorite chair. I know every detail of the story; I can feel every emotion, smell every familiar scent. My challenge is to create a world for these poems outside of my mind where others can share my memories. When they look at one of my poems I would like readers to feel comfortable and want to answer back, to open up their photo album, to tell me their stories.

MEMORY

Sitting on a musty recliner
during my first visit to Italy
I decided to memorize the room
instead of taking a picture.
Six years later I can't even remember
my brother's face the day he died.

Milton Kessler and his
daughter Paula.

Milton Kessler's son Dan, daughter Paula, and son Dave.

MILTON
KESSLER
1930–2000

Sometimes, in the middle of my day, I would get a phone call from my dad thousands of miles away. "I want to read you something," he would say, his beautiful voice singing with excitement. So whatever I was doing I stopped, and I settled myself to listen. He would read me a new poem, and we would talk about it . . . about the music of it, about the words, sometimes each word, and it was wonderful. I loved those calls. Each time I felt like I was being invited into an amazingly precious world . . . a world of poetry and of family.

On May 9, 1960, I was born on my father's thirtieth birthday. I was early, my mom says, but I think I was right on time. It makes sense that I was born on that day.

I can't remember when I first realized what a poet was, but I always knew my dad was one. A poet, I thought, was someone who carried around a notebook, scribbling lines and thoughts. A poet was someone who was around for breakfast, was there when we got home from school, and sat among us every night at our family dinners. A poet was with us for every family trip and adventure. A poet was someone who spent many hours a day with his students and colleagues at the university, and the rest of the time with us, his family . . . talking, laughing, dreaming.

Growing up, often I'd wake up in the middle of the night, and I would hear the snapping sounds of Dad's typewriter downstairs in the kitchen. I felt great comfort knowing he was there, writing, as the rest of the family slept . . . Mom, Dave, and Dan. It was as if our world, our family world, was the nourishment, the core, of his poetry world. At least I like to think so.

PAULA N. KESSLER

BALLAD FOR DAVE

Driving south in sleet
I know you're coming north.
Take it easy son,
whatever road you're on.

Hope the old car's safe.
Pray you stay awake.
Take it easy son,
whatever road you're on.

Watch the ice at Great Bend.
Gear down in the dark.
Take it easy son,
whatever road you're on.

Don't pass trucks downhill.
Keep the music off.
Stay away from ghosts.
Stay away from thoughts.

Something sees us both
turning toward our town.
Take it easy son,
whatever road you're on.

PLAIN POPLAR

And he said, "Fuck you, fuck you," he said. "You're no good."
And I said, "Bullshit, you're full of shit," I said.
And he came over his body shaking with violated
                                        commandment
and raised his spotted smoky fist and said,
                                        "I'm going to do
something you won't like if you say that,"
                                        and I smirked at 220,
and was afraid of my father's great trembling,

                        and he was "1898," Oh Lord,
            he was 98 pounds,
        and he raised his fist on
                            his breast
                                    bone,

        and after went in
            and put his arm over his eyes,
        and I saw it, my God,
                and it was no one else I saw
but the strength of my Pop.

And, yes, he set his paper down and raised his fist again.

Oh washed facebrow unfrozen on a sill of poplar,
no make-up, a man a man, your perfect silver curls,
moist under the shroud, is the beauty of my father,
                              and I reached in
                    and touched your fist
                                                again.
              "Oh Dad is dead, Mom, Dad is dead."
And he got from his chair
                         stiff and true
              after I said, "bullshit,"
     and he came
all wind in his shirt
                    and wet pants
              and sour twenty dollar bills
       and acid rubber bands and pencils
and brought his quick fist

              reflexes snapping
in my bewildered, joyous eyes,
                    his fist
                            all taped, cracked
              and cigar elegant,
                         his back
                    arced
       as the Jewish prince he was,
                         "Just call me Artie."

And "Fuck you," he said, "fuck you."

"You always take your mother's side."

And he came

right over at 87

and cash,

gelt,

that was it,

"You're a miser, I said, "You think poor."

"You're full of shit," he said.

"Get a housekeeper," I said.

"I'd rather jump

out the window," he said.

"Dad is dead, Mom,

Dad is dead,"

God damn it, Dad.

Your eyes right to the pegs

where the box closed,

and your chest bones

peaceful

and proud

and strong.

Pow Pop! Pow Pop!

And his mouth made

"I love you I love you."

                        "Soon I will take a trip
                on a train." (smile)
      "Maybe tomorrow it will be better," (smile)
            "a little better," (smile)
            "a little better," (smile).

O Pop, who will curse your newspaper now?
"Why don't you ever wear a suit?" he said.
"What kind of a man are you?" he said.
What a shot, Pop, what a shot.
                    Pow Pop! Pow Pop!

SECRET LOVE

My father's back
heaves toward the sea,

and the stripes of his shirt
pull toward his right wrist,

which clerked mail into the boxes
and carried coffee for the bosses.

Now he needs a firm pillow to rest
the ache against as he reads

in his loveseat, summer and winter,
the lamp by his good shoulder.

Yet watch him bend at night to lock
the stick of Judah in the terrace door

or hear his tenor soar against the president
and injustice to the poor.

He is secure on his pension. He does not
use a cane at 84 or face the floor.

This is the back I lay beside in secret peace
during the dark daytimes after my

humiliation at school and before his invisible
war of work. He sleeps well still in flannel.

Thanks Pop, and I touch his silky back. Then he
dresses to go out. We worry a bit more.

Today, my mother thought to reassure
and said, You'll live to be a hundred.

I will if you will, he said.
They shook on it.

Maxine Kumin with brothers Peter and Herbert on left,
Fred on right, circa 1930 in Germantown, Pennsylvania.

MAXINE
KUMIN

As for my great-grandfather, Elias Rosenberg, family lore says that at age sixteen, he came across the Atlantic on a sailing vessel, landed at Baltimore in 1848, and as an itinerant peddler set out for Virginia. He sewed uniforms for Confederate soldiers in the Civil War, prospered as a dry-goods merchant in Radford, then a very small town. Alas, there is no picture of him. My next-older brother was originally named Edward Elias, in memory of our great-grandfather, but insisted at age six that his name be changed to Peter Jr., which actually took place.

We all pestered our mother for any tidbit of information from her girlhood in rural Virginia, which seemed historical and exotic to us in suburban Philadelphia. There were twelve children in her family; she was number six. Everyone had a job. She had to tend the chickens and gather the eggs, and she hated the way they pecked at her feet and flapped their wings in her face. People went everywhere by horse and carriage; she remembered a white harness for Sundays. (I can't imagine this; what would it have been made of?) And of course there was a pony, a succession of ponies, which is probably how it all began for me.

FOR MY GREAT-GRANDFATHER:
A MESSAGE LONG OVERDUE

You with the beard as red as Barbarossa's
uncut from its first sprouting to the hour
they tucked it in your belt and closed your eyes,
you with the bright brass water pipe, a surefire
plaything under the neighbors' children's noses
for you to puff and them to idolize

—the pipe you'd packed up out of somewhere
in Bohemia, along with the praying shawl
and the pair of little leather praying boxes—
Great-Grandfather, old blue-eyed fox of foxes,
I have three pages of you. That is all.

1895. A three-page letter
from Newport News, Virginia, written
on your bleached-out bills of sale under the stern
heading: ROSENBERG THE TAILOR, DEBTOR,
A FULL LINE OF GOODS OF ALL THE LATEST IN
SUITING AND PANTS. My mother has just been born.

You write to thank your daughter for the picture
of that sixth grandchild. There are six more to come.
"My heart's tenderest tendrils" is your style.

"God bless you even as He blessed Jacob." Meanwhile
you stitch the year away in Christendom.

Meanwhile it seems you've lost your wife, remarried
a girl your daughter's age and caused distress.
"It was a cold relentless hand of Death
that scattered us abroad," you write, "robbing us
of Wife and Mother." Grieving for that one buried
you send new wedding pictures now herewith
and close with *mazel* and *brocha,* words that bless.

The second bride lived on in one long study
of pleats and puckers to the age of ninety-two,
smoked cigarettes, crocheted and spoke of you
to keep our kinship threaded up and tidy.

Was that the message—the erratic ways
the little lore that has been handed on
suffers, but sticks it out in the translation?
I tell you to my children, who forget,
are brimful of themselves, and anyway
might have preferred a farmer or a sailor,
but you and I are buttoned, flap to pocket.
Welcome, ancestor, Rosenberg the Tailor!
I choose to be a lifetime in your debt.

Stanley Kunitz.

Stanley's mother, Yetta Jasspon Kunitz, 1951.

Stanley's daughter, Gretchen Kunitz, summer 1977.

STANLEY
KUNITZ

One of my mother's gifts to me during my high school years in Worcester, Massachusetts, was a green and gold set of Tolstoy's works in the standard translation of that period. I could not decide which volume I should read first. As I was leafing through the books on the table, a single provocative sentence in *Anna Karenina* jumped off the page and ended my search:

> *Happy families are all alike; every unhappy family*
> *is unhappy in its own way.*

In other words (if anyone dared say them), unhappy families are more interesting, distinctive, and inherently creative than their boring opposites.

That wild-eyed, bearded Russian, I sensed, was speaking directly to me, as great writers have a way of doing in their encounters; and he was telling me not to brood: My fate was mine to make.

I can see clearly now that if it had not been for my mother, we could never have survived as a family. She was a woman of formidable will and pride and honor, staunch heart, and razor-sharp intelligence, whose only school was the sweatshops of New York, where she had toiled before moving to Worcester for her marriage.

In 1905, when I was born, she was still in shock from the cruel loss of my father only a few weeks before. Left bankrupt, with me and my two older sisters to support, she opened a street-corner dry-goods store, where she sewed garments in the back room, sometimes deep into the night. Only a few years later, she emerged as an innovative designer and manufacturer of children's dresses, occupying a capacious loft humming with machines. She must have been one of the first women to run a business of that scale in the country.

I knew little about her origins until, shortly before her death at eighty-six, she wrote for me, at my request, a memoir that vividly recalls her early years in "a Godforsaken village of three hundred families" in her native Lithuania:

> *To be poor in those days was more than an inconvenience, it was also a disgrace. I hated small-town life with all its discomforts, its public bathhouse open once a week for women, mud more than a foot deep in rainy weather, ignorance and superstition around you, everyone watching everything you did. I decided to go to America.*

She left in August 1890, crossing the German border at night, since she had no passport, and made her way to the city of Antwerp, her port of embarkation, lugging two heavy wicker baskets that contained all her worldly possessions, including hopefully her trousseau.

You would never guess, from the clarity of her observations and the specificity of her details, that my mother had no notes or documents at hand with which to refresh her memory of events that belonged to another world, almost another age. Her account of her arrival in this country as a steerage passenger, deep in the hold of the Red Star liner *Rhineland*, evokes the bravery of her spirit at the end of an arduous journey and the beginning of a new life:

> *At 9:30 A.M. on September 22, 1890, we passed the Statue of Liberty and docked at Castle Garden. It happened to be my twenty-fourth anniversary, but the day I landed in America was the day of my rebirth and my real birthday.*

JOURNAL FOR MY DAUGHTER

1

Your turn. Grass of confusion.
You say you had a father once:
his name was absence.
He left, but did not let you go.
Part of him, more than a shadow,
beckoned down corridors,
secret, elusive, saturnine,
melting at your touch.
In the crack
of a divided house
grew the resentment-weed.
It has white inconspicuous flowers.
Family of anthologists!
Collectors of injuries!

2

I wake to a glittering world,
to the annunciation of the frost.
A popeyed chipmunk scurries past,
the pockets of his cheeks bulging.
As the field mice store seeds,
as the needle-nosed shrew

threading under the woodpile
deposits little heaps of land-snails
for milestones on its runways,
I propose
that we gather our affections.
Lambkin, I care.

3

I was happy you were born,
your banks of digits
equipped for decimals,
and all your clever parts
neatly in place.
Your nation gives me joy,
as it has always given.
If I could have my choice
on the way to exile
I think I'd rather sleep forever
than wake up cold
in a country without women.

4

You cried. You cried.
You wasted and you cried.
Night after night
I walked the floor with you,

croaking the same old
tranquillizing song,
the only tune
I ever learned to carry.
In the rosy tissue
of your brain,
where memory begins,
that theme is surely scored,
waiting till you need
to play it back.
There were three crows
sat on a tree
Sing Billy Magee Magaw.
You do not need to sing to me.
I like the sound of your voice
even when you phone from school
asking for money.

5

There was a big blond uncle-bear,
wounded, smoke-eyed, wild,
who shambled from the west
with his bags full of havoc.
He spoke the bears' grunt-language,
waving his paws
and rocking on his legs.

Both of us were drunk,
slapping each other on the back,
sweaty with genius.
He spouted his nonsense-rhymes,
roaring like a behemoth.
You crawled under the sofa.

6

Goodies are shaken
from the papa-tree:
Be what you are. Give
what is yours to give.
Have style. Dare.
Such a storm of fortune cookies!
Outside your room
stands the white-headed prowler
in his multiple disguises
who reminds you of your likeness.
Wherever you turn,
down whatever street,
in the fugues of appetite,
in the groin of nightmare,
he waits for you,
haggard with his thousand years.
His agents are everywhere,
his heart is at home

in your own generation;
the folded message in his hands
is stiff with dirt and wine-stains,
older than the Dead Sea Scrolls.
Daughter, read:
What do I want of my life?
More! More!

7

Demonstrations in the streets.
I am there not there,
ever uneasy in a crowd.
But you belong,
flaunting your home-made
insubordinate flag.
Why should I be surprised?
We come of a flinty maverick line.
In my father's time, I'm told,
our table was set in turn
for Maxim Gorky, Emma Goldman,
and the atheist Ingersoll.
If your slogan is mis-spelt
Don't tred on me!
still it strikes
parents and politicians down.

Noli me tangere! is what
I used to cry in Latin once.
Oh to be radical, young, desirable, cool!

8

Your first dog was a Pekinese,
fat and saucy Ko-San,
half mandarin, half mini-lion,
who chased milkmen and mailmen
and bit the tires of every passing car
till a U.S. Royal bit him back.
You sobbed for half an hour,
then romped to the burial service
in the lower garden
by the ferny creek.
I helped you pick the stones
to mark his shallow grave.
It was the summer I went away.
One night I carried you outdoors,
in a blitz of fireflies,
to watch your first eclipse.
Your far-off voice,
drugged with milk and sleep,
said it was a leaf
sliding over the light.

9

The night when Coleridge,
heavy-hearted,
bore his crying child outside,
he noted
that those brimming eyes
caught the reflection
of the starry sky,
and each suspended tear
made a sparkling moon.

"Journal for My Daughter" was written during the period of student rebellion and mass demonstrations provoked by the Vietnam War. The "uncle-bear" in Part 5 is an evocation of my poet friend, the late Theodore Roethke, on one of his visits in the early fifties. Gretchen Kunitz is a physician who lives on the West Coast with her husband and two daughters. In a talk before a professional audience, she has referred to "Journal for My Daughter" as an important contributor to her development and self-understanding.

MY MOTHER'S PEARS

Plump, green-gold, Worcester's pride,
    transported through autumn skies
        in a box marked Handle With Care

sleep eighteen Bartlett pears,
    hand-picked and polished and packed
        for deposit at my door,

each in its crinkled nest
    with a stub of stem attached
        and a single bright leaf like a flag.

A smaller than usual crop,
    but still enough to share with me,
        as always at harvest time.

Those strangers are my friends
    whose kindness blesses the house
        my mother built at the edge of town

beyond the last trolley-stop
    when the century was young, and she
        proposed, for her children's sake,

to marry again, not knowing how soon
    the windows would grow dark
        and the velvet drapes come down.

Rubble accumulates in the yard,
    workmen are hammering on the roof,
        I am standing knee-deep in dirt

with a shovel in my hand.
    Mother has wrapped a kerchief round her head,
        her glasses glint in the sun.

When my sisters appear on the scene,
    gangly and softly tittering,
        she waves them back into the house

to fetch us pails of water,
    and they skip out of our sight
        in their matching middy blouses.

I summon up all my strength
    to set the pear tree in the ground,
        unwinding its burlap shroud.

It is taller than I. "Make room
    for the roots!" my mother cries,
        "Dig the hole deeper."

"My Mother's Pears" is dedicated to Carol and Greg Stockmal, of Worcester, Massachusetts, who own and occupy the house my mother built. Their annual gift of pears from the backyard inspired this poem. I think of Carol and Greg as members of our extended family.

Greg Kuzma with his wife, son, and daughter.

GREG
KUZMA

Three years ago I was reading a biography of the poet Robert Frost, and I had to stop when I came to the years where Frost's children begin to suffer and die. I was myself a rather natural writer, and I could write all day and night forever. Not that I thought I would ever achieve Frost's success or popularity, but I suddenly became aware of what one might think to be the cost of fame. Closing the book, I made a decision not to become another self-absorbed, reckless writer, who makes a ruin around himself, or who betrays the people he loves or ought to love. Actually my soul-searching was unnecessary. Within a few years my brother Jeff died in a car crash, and I became a bad father anyway, my whole energy—like that of someone in Alcoholics Anonymous training—taken up with *not* drinking myself into a stupor or living in despair.

Yet I think that reading the Frost book marked a real turn for me. A wide turn, which I am still in the process of making. To a very real extent, being a smart-aleck poet is over for me. If anything, now I want only to tell the truth, however raw or unvarnished. When Jeff died I knew beyond any doubt that I would give up every syllable I had ever written or spoken to bring him back to life.

In the face of this loss, I keep now a measure of what is meaningful to me. I have even come to believe that the writing which detaches itself from simple and homely truths is a cruel and unconscionable art. As the poet Hayden Carruth said a few years ago, "To be a good poet, you have to be a good person."

To be a good person is both a daily task and a lifelong work. If poems happen along the way, or screenplays, I will be happy for them. But I will never put poetry before family ever again.

MY SON SKATING ON DOANE'S LAKE

A silver sky, and the lake silver.
And Mark, you skate with your short stride,
the dark skates glinting on their wide blades.
It is a small frame you are, a thin dim figure,
pathetic in a huge scarf, red-cheeked,
wearing huge brown gloves, ragged,
which your mother cast off,
wearing upon your face the twin marks of our love
my nose, her eyes,
and the mouth enlarged through both of ours.
You are all that I love in a man's body,
doing your little work of bone and flesh,
another of your life's days.

*Rich Landers (on far right, bottom) with his sister
and grandparents, 1991.*

RICH
LANDERS

A poem can spring from a story or a relationship or the memory of a phrase. Many vivid and formative experiences come from the home and those first significant relationships that seem to crop up even when I'm trying to write about other things. A genuine return to such events brings on a certain emotional vulnerability and offers new forms of speech and description.

My family always had books around the house, including several volumes that gave me my first introduction to poetry.

GENESIS

My mother gave birth to me and I never once thanked her,
never once looked up into the cement chamber where my sister
     read, to mark an unusual fondness,
and gratitude was due for whoever took my prepubescence to its
     dry end.

I'm thinking of people I've seen emptied, never to be mentioned.
The girl who changed into swimwear for me in the apartment
     across the street.
As we spoke over the phone, her number written in large letters
     through the window,

or a year later, walking together the length of a street,
not once did I have the grace to thank her before moving away,
this trace of humanity, traveling toward another sworn secret.

Shara McCallum with her grandmother and grandfather.

SHARA McCALLUM

I was born and grew up as a young child in Jamaica. Many of my poems, like "Wolves," come out of those early experiences of understanding the world around me, and myself in relation to that world. Like this one, many are also set in Jamaica and reflect its landscape—the river up in the mountain; the seashore and clear blue waters; coconut trees, mango trees, roses, plumbago, hibiscus. . . . Many of my poems include another sense of Jamaica through the sounds of the language. A *duppy* in Jamaica is a ghost or spirit of the dead. My grandfather, the Papa of the poem, in teasing me about the wolves, uses the kind of voice we take on when we tell scary tales or "*duppy* stories" to someone else to playfully frighten them. "Wolves" is also similar to several of my other poems in that it is about the relationship between a grown-up and child, about the complexity of love and trust between them.

WOLVES

for my grandfather

Once when night was as black
as the inside of a calabash
and the only light on the verandah
came from the inside rooms
spilling out, the dogs began to howl
to an imagined moon.
Those are wolves, you said,
in the same voice I'd heard
duppy stories told before.
And my eyes did not move
from the dark beyond the grill.
Inching backward across the cold floor,
finding your leg at last
pressed against my back,
I reached behind and wrapped
my small arms around the trunk
of your calf, hoisting
my body up. For days,
months, even years after,
I would still ask—
There are no wolves in Jamaica,
right, Papa?—forcing you

to repeat the half truth uttered
one moonless night
to allay the fears of a child:
There are no wolves in Jamaica, Shara.
No wolves in Jamaica.

Margaret K. Menges with her sons, Daniel and David.

MARGARET K. MENGES

My mother was a teacher, is still a teacher. Her mother, Agnes Ryan, was a nurse, and her grandmother, Katie Ellen Calligan, sewed linen shirtwaists for the fancy ladies in town. Her great-grandmother, Maggie Quinn, made the trip from Ireland alone when she was twelve and had enough money to get to a town called Little Meadows in upstate New York. My mother is the inheritor of their strengths. When she would come home from school when we were kids, she'd continually remind us, "When I make a right-hand turn off Church Street to Larchmont Road, I want this place to be a refuge, a sanctuary." And it was.

The world baffles us with its sorrow and chaos. I want things to make sense for my sons here in these rooms we share so that they can find their way later on as adults. This is the sweet-heavy burden of family. My hope is that they both will be able to live within themselves surely enough to begin self-forgetting. Rilke said, "Being here is so much." Writing poems helps me remember this.

My mother taught me, teaches me, to pay attention to things—light, children, seasons—all the wild possibilities of life.

FOR ANGELA

Angela's coming for dinner, he said and
he bought the card with flowers and red hearts
flashing in circles.
He set the card under the rose light
on the dining room table,
next to the bills and the junk mail
piled there in the daily hubbub
which we promptly cleared away
        because
Angela, Angela's coming, he said.
and it made me laugh to remember
and I thought it'd be swell to have a theme,
like a national holiday for young love, so
we had Angel-hair pasta and Angel food cake,
white and full of air, whipped cream
and strawberries redder than roses and
blood and fairy-tale apples.
Angela, Angela . . . she arrived like the
Fourth of July and sat at the
end of the table, staring into
the blue eyes of the boy I've known forever.

THE WINTER OF STORIES

Tucking you in, blanketing you
those winter nights while snow
fell relentlessly past our dark
windowed reflections, I believed
that words, the worlds they built,
could insulate us,
so it was the winter of stories—
tales of summer worlds filled
with grinning children swinging
over muddy rivers to mosquitoes' hum.

That winter of stories,
we read *Huck Finn,* drifted each
night on the Mississippi
with Huck and Jim. . . . I'd mark
the page and leave you there
on the raft, under a huge prairie sky.
Then, in the darkness, you'd listen while,
downstairs, I played the piano,
requests only, those you'd call down.
Never, Never Land or *I Can Fly* and
I'd play until you fell asleep, the
Mississippi spilling into the sandy
blue of Pirates' Cove.

What did this have to do
with the man behind the closed door,
sleeping, holding the dark bottle,
the television droning on?
I would wait until the local
news came on, the next day's weather
forecast—checking storms from the south,
wind chill factors—and then I'd try
to wake him up, tell him it was time to
go to bed.

Tonight, years away, miles away
from that house and those rooms,
home from college, you ask me to play
the piano before you fall asleep,
something classical, you say.
And here I am, still, making
lullabies the only way I know.

It might be miles beyond
the moon or right there where you stand.
The song, the answer, it's right
here where we stand and we
can't always keep everyone with us.

Jerry Mirskin and his son, Noah.

Jerry Mirskin and his father.

JERRY
MIRSKIN

As I look over my recent poems, I'm aware that much of my work speaks to themes of parenthood, childhood, rootedness, and family. If I had to explain why, I'd say that as a person and writer, I have the primary goal of self-knowledge. It's my sense that we know ourselves to the extent to which we can appreciate our relationships with the world. Being a child, or a parent, or a family member represents primary relationships, and many of my poems begin with those who first described the world to me. My parents and grandparents are coordinates in my life. Stars in my constellation. The words *mother, father, brother, grandmother,* and *son* are tokens that have universal and personal meaning.

However, the world I inherit as I listen to the stories of my relatives' lives is not entirely my world. My work often begins with where my family came from, what their lives are or were like, and how my life is similar and different. I try to make sense of where I fit in. Because versions of the world are passed from generation to generation in language, poetry is a natural medium in which new ways of seeing the world can occur. It's also the medium in which we acknowledge the lives of those who have contributed to our own. Poetry can do that. It can say, "Wow, that was really hard" or "That was wonderful" in a new and meaningful way. It can say, "Thank you."

MY FATHER

Pop sees me
come back from the after life.
A small night table light guards
his orbiting. He's reading and says,
How was it? I'm always coming down
from my old room, looking in
taking his smile for a smile, a promise
that he won't grow old without me.
He's reading an archaeology book
and a history book. I imagine
in one there's a people who knew
a thing that was hard to look at,
and in the other, on every page
he finds that they were doing
the best they could.

When I see my father lying in bed, reading
I want to pass by and say,
Be my happy father.

ERRATUM

The last nine lines of Jerry Mirskin's poem "Bronx Park East" (on pages 119 to 121) were included in error. The poem will appear corrected in subsequent printings of Roots and Flowers *and is included here.*

BRONX PARK EAST

My grandmother gives me a glass of cold water,
I say out loud.
My uncle wants to know if it's a poem.
She's from Russia.
She gives me what I wanted.
Is it a poem?
Did she come here to give you a glass of water?
My uncle is cantankerous.
Seventy years old,
and we're sitting in the kitchen
of the apartment in which he grew up.
I wanted a glass of water,
and I wanted to say something true.
For that you have to open your mouth
and say it, and see how it sounds.
This is the apartment in which my father
and my aunt grew up.
The one from which my father and uncle left
to go into service during the war.
The same they returned to, to find their father gone.
If they wanted a glass of water
they probably got it for themselves.
I know that's what he's thinking.
They didn't wait for Grandma to push by the table.
They didn't watch her shuttle from stove
to refrigerator, to sink, and back to table.
They just went and got it.
It wasn't a poem.
This has been her home since he was a boy.
His hands on the same table for sixty years.
When my grandmother hands me the glass
I feel that I'm among them.
I'm his brother. She's my mother. She smiles at me.
I should say, On me.
The Yiddish word is *kvell.* You say, She *kvells* on me.

Though it's not something you say about yourself.
I want to say,
My grandmother gives me a glass of cold water.
And maybe reveal how she smiles at me
with all the light of her kitchen
in her well-traveled eyes.
Eyes that left Russia when she was twelve.
Eyes that left behind her mother and father
the people she loved, the acres and the hours
she spent in her home.
My uncle is cantankerous,
but that doesn't mean anything.
Sixty years in the same apartment,
people ask her how she feels.

My grandmother gives me a glass of cold water.

BRONX PARK EAST

My grandmother gives me a glass of cold water,
I say out loud.
My uncle wants to know if it's a poem.
She's from Russia.
She gives me what I wanted.
Is it a poem?
Did she come here to give you a glass of water?
My uncle is cantankerous.
Seventy years old,
and we're sitting in the kitchen
of the apartment in which he grew up.
I wanted a glass of water,
and I wanted to say something true.
For that you have to open your mouth
and say it, and see how it sounds.
This is the apartment in which my father
and my aunt grew up.
The one from which my father and uncle left
to go into service during the war.
The same they returned to, to find their father gone.
If they wanted a glass of water
they probably got it for themselves.
I know that's what he's thinking.
They didn't wait for Grandma to push by the table.
They didn't watch her shuttle from stove

to refrigerator, to sink, and back to table.
They just went and got it.
It wasn't a poem.
This has been her home since he was a boy.
His hands on the same table for sixty years.
When my grandmother hands me the glass
I feel that I'm among them.
I'm his brother. She's my mother. She smiles at me.
I should say, On me.
The Yiddish word is *kvell*. You say, She *kvells* on me.
Though it's not something you say about yourself.
I want to say,
My grandmother gives me a glass of cold water.
And maybe reveal how she smiles at me
with all the light of her kitchen
in her well-traveled eyes.
Eyes that left Russia when she was twelve.
Eyes that left behind her mother and father
the people she loved, the acres and the hours
she spent in her home.
My uncle is cantankerous,
but that doesn't mean anything.
Sixty years in the same apartment,
people ask her how she feels.

My grandmother gives me a glass of cold water.
My son's head rests
sleeping on my shoulder.

And I know
what others have known.
And no one will blame me
if I give everything I have
to him, who runs at me—
who lets me for a while
into his dream.

Greg Moglia.

Greg's father.

GREG
MOGLIA

Italian-American families eat well, tell stories to one another. Smile and eat some more. But poetry? Not too often. But it was there *all the time*. We knew it was family. But did not say. And so in my poems a hint of what happened. Sometimes a hint is enough.

ON THAT DAY

So Dad, my brother said
I know why you are sending us to college
You want to look good
Be able to say
My boys college grads

All on a warm summer day
My brother giving me
My first lesson in courage
Ask even when it hurts

My father giving me
My first lesson in poetry
The look on his face

My father on that day
Giving me my first lesson in love
In his silence
My first lesson in love

PIETRO

At five I stood amazed watching this lion of a man
Become a scribbling child before the hardened paper
Of his social security check

Blistered muscled fingers fought to form each letter
Until in scrambled lines
Pietro

My grandfather Italian immigrant slave to the construction company
Dad said the boss loved him did the work of two maybe three men
But I want you to see him at eighty

Watch him tour the neighborhood garbage gather the newspapers
Stack them under each arm until the load too large
He bound them in twine found a lonely plank as a lever
And wandered home

Piled the papers in the garage where they stood until Saturday
When his grandsons would cart the hundreds of pounds
To the junkman where they gained a dollar or two

And one grandson now at fifty-five
Believed so in his grandfather's discipline
Played his role as teacher

Spending all day marking one set of papers
Never missing a day of class
Working through colds and family battles

Till one morning came the need to finally rest to stop
To take his heart in his hand
Scribble the pained awkward lines

What have you lived?
Learned?
And he could barely write his name

Kyoko Mori
with her mother, Takako.

Kyoko Mori (back row, left) with her aunts Keiko and Michiyo,
her uncle Shiro, her brother Jumpli (front row), and cousins
Eiko, Yuniko, Yukiko, and Takeshi.

KYOKO MORI

Although now I am a few years older than my mother ever was, I still think of myself as her daughter. Childhood is like an old house we keep going back to. It's the place where we learned the names of colors and shapes, the way our mother's garden flowers drooped in the rain, the sound of the noon siren, the warmth of the kitchen floor in front of our oven.

Sometimes, we revisit our childhood and notice things we hadn't noticed when we were actually children. To know and write about any place, you have to go away, and then you have to come back. Writing comes from a combination of being rooted and being uprooted. I've spent twenty years in Japan, twenty-two years in the American Midwest, and now I am on the East Coast. I feel rooted and uprooted in the right amount.

Of course, no matter how many towns and places we've gotten to know through our moving and traveling, there will always be towns and countries—and experiences, too—that we have never visited. To me, becoming a parent is like a country I have not visited.

SEEING MY PARENTS IN NEW YORK

At "Peking Duck" in Chinatown
my stepmother sucks
white noodles, scrapes

shrimp off her plate.
New York is too dirty,
she says, every street

infested with beggars. My
father eats in silence, pulls
out his shirt-tail to

fan his chest in public. Food
makes him sweat. He bites
the fortune cookie in half,

spits out his fortune
chewed up and unreadable.
I slide back thirteen

years into their kitchen,
clench my teeth on the crystal
goblet and spit out

the shards into the sink
with my blood, eat
nothing but the ice in my

water and wish I could
turn transparent—
resign myself

finger by finger into
thin air. My father pays
the bill. He's got seven

hundred bucks in his
wallet. At the Sheraton, my
stepmother shows me her

paper underwear she can
flush into the toilet—
no soil tangled into her

immaculate suitcase. At dusk
I leave them in the rain
headed for some Broadway

show where they'll stare
at bright lights
comprehending nothing.

UNCLES

The first in seven years, my uncle Shiro's
letter is full of names, paragraph after
paragraph of brief synopsis like a list of
characters from a novel I could never
finish. He omits his two sisters though

the brothers get a paragraph each after his
children. Uncle Ken teaches chemistry
at a high school. Uncle Yasuo made money
on stocks; he goes fishing on weekends. Every
summer, they meet at their mother's house to

drink beer and talk into night clinking amber
glasses while cicadas buzz with heat and moths
flutter over purple lantern flowers. The room,
blurred with smoke, is unchanged. From the cupboard, they
take out the hundred round stones for the Japanese

chess game they wanted to teach me twenty
years ago. Blind to the patterns in black
and white, I never knew if I was winning or
losing. I cannot now imagine their
talk except that we women figure little. There's

no time to tell my uncles what I
remember most about them: the purple
hair of the doll Shiro gave me on the day of
his marriage, Ken hitting the volleyball
to me so hard my wrist zinged, the green

feathers of the nightingales Yasuo
kept in bamboo cages. Child of the dead
sister whose name they avoid, I can write
nothing but news, remarks about weather.
It is fall in Wisconsin; red maple leaves

brighten the lawn like stitches in a quilt.
Even inside my house, the potted
avocado has shed one long leaf, its
smooth lines like the fish in the river
at home, where black crows gather another season

over the leafless branches of the persimmon
tree, the silent bells of bitter
fruit. My uncles, as you harvest the fruit to
dry, to sweeten in the sun, remember my mother
who sang you to sleep under the quilts.

Tell me a story I have forgotten.

Megeen Mulholland and her brother Brendan.

MEGEEN
MULHOLLAND

My father died when I was very young, so everything I know about him has been passed on to me by my family. For years my mother, sisters, and brothers repeated stories about my father till I was old enough to tell them myself. I've added to this family tradition with my own retellings.

This may or may not reflect events exactly as they occurred. Many times the experiences portrayed in my poems are the way I alone perceive them or wish them to be. If my brothers or sisters were to write their versions of the same events, theirs might differ greatly from my own.

I take pride and comfort in being a member of a large Irish family and in drawing upon its colorful history to create "snapshots" in which we can see variations of ourselves and our relationships to one another. For a writer, the theme of family is always compelling, and each new development provides me with a fresh approach.

OUR FATHER'S IMAGE

Thought young for the funeral,
my brother Brendan and I
stayed with neighbors
for hours in our own house
until our mother returned
in a black car,
wearing black fur,
her hands smelling
deep of earth,
and more lightly
of flowers,
the scent lingering like
the voices of a choir
after hymn;
Sunday, the saints
stood arched in the church windows—
their halos shining in noon sun,
and on his young blond head
at midnight, in moonlight
as Brendan slept—
his head against the pillow,
under the pale sheets,
his arms crossed over his chest
with the earnest fists
on his shoulders,

as if holding himself down
in our father's image,
for fear of rising,
a boy.

Howard Nelson holding his daughter Tess (at left) with his son Zach; his wife, Stephanie; and his daughter Sarah.

HOWARD NELSON

Having a family is a big responsibility and a big blessing. As everyone knows, it can cause a lot of stress and frustration and ache, but it can also bring the deepest comfort, satisfaction, and happiness.

Poetry can be hard, and sometimes writing it seems impossible—but it also brings the deepest comfort, satisfaction, and happiness. So that's one connection between poetry and family.

Being somebody's child, and then later being a parent to a child yourself—what could be more common yet mysterious than that? That's another way that poetry and family are connected: in poems and in life, what seems ordinary is actually of vast importance and mystery.

My third child, Tess, was born when her sister and brother, Sarah and Zack, were fifteen and twelve, so in a way my wife and I got to do it all over again, with the help of older kids who were a little—but not too much, just enough—like parents themselves. When we were pregnant with Tess, I felt excited and amazed, and I wrote a book of poems about it. Usually poems come slowly for me, but during that time I wrote them out one after another.

WEARINESS

She comes home tired from work,
and tired from carrying that big belly around.
She strips to her underwear and socks
and flops (carefully, in three stages)
down on the bed,
arms out from her sides, palms upturned,
legs spraddled,
and closes her eyes.
At the center, the round mountain
with its little crater,
bellybutton stretched flat,
just a small, round scar.
In a minute, she's breathing
heavy and slow.
She gives a little moan.
She looks as if she carries
the burden of the world in her belly.
Well, it's true:
a human being is carried there.

IN THE CLASS FOR GIVING BIRTH

Have you ever been in a room where there are ten pregnant women?
It's like looking up one night and seeing ten full moons glowing in
the sky!

*Naomi Shihab Nye and her son,
Madison, in 1987.*

Naomi Shihab Nye, age 8, and her father.

NAOMI
SHIHAB NYE

As a child, I would stand on our front-porch step in St. Louis, watching light sift through trees, falling onto grass, tulips, and sidewalk. I could hear my mother in the kitchen, the sound a spoon made in the dish drainer when it touched other spoons, the clang of pans and clink of plates. Sometimes my mother sang as she worked—I held that song as I held my own breath. Soon my father would turn the corner in the blue Buick, and my family would sit down to eat at the small table, looking out through screens into the evening.

I felt haunted by the simple beauty of this even as I lived it. Couldn't we slow it all down? Couldn't we be as calm as the cherry trees in the yard? Our days were racing past. Too much to organize, experience, weave together. This was my mystery. I wept, turning three, because I did not feel done with two.

Poetry helped me stand back from the racing life and look at it longer. Words were the quiet, twining roots, the true gravity. Poetry enables all the worlds within and without to feel more noticed, remarked upon, savored. Poetry helped me feel a center inside which could always be slow if it wanted to be.

It saved me and continues to save me to this day.

Now I am holding on to someone else's early time—our son's. At twelve, he zooms forward enthusiastically toward thirteen. I would like each day to be ten times longer. I would treasure more pauses between things, more margins, more spaciousness in every day's arrangement.

But still, only poetry lets that be.

WEDDING CAKE

Once on a plane
a woman asked me to hold her baby
and disappeared.
I figured it was safe,
our being on a plane and all.
How far could she go?

She returned one hour later,
having changed her clothes
and washed her hair.
I didn't recognize her.

By this time the baby
and I had examined
each other's necks.
We had cried a little.
I had a silver bracelet
and a watch.
Gold studs glittered
in the baby's ears.
She wore a tiny white dress
leafed with layers
like a wedding cake.

I did not want
to give her back.

The baby's curls coiled tightly
against her scalp,
another alphabet.
I read *new new new.*
My mother gets tired.
I'll chew your hand.

The baby left my skirt crumpled,
my lap aching.
Now I'm her secret guardian,
the little nub of dream
that rises slightly
but won't come clear.

As she grows,
as she feels ill at ease,
I'll bob my knee.

What will she forget?
Whom will she marry?
He'd better check with me.
I'll say once she flew
dressed like a cake
between two doilies of cloud.
She could slip the card into a pocket,
pull it out.
Already she knew the small finger
was funnier than the whole arm.

HOW FAR IS IT TO THE LAND WE LEFT?

On the first day of his life
the baby opens his eyes
and gets tired doing even that.
He cries when they place a cap on his head.
Too much, too much!

Later the whole world will touch him
and he won't even flinch.

GENETICS

From my father I have inherited the ability
to stand in a field and stare.

Look, look at that gray dot by the fence.
It's his donkey. My father doesn't have
a deep interest in donkeys, more a figurative one.
To know it's out there nuzzling the ground.

That's how I feel about my life.
I like to skirt the edges. There it is in the field.
Feeding itself.

•

From my mother, an obsession about the stove
and correct spelling. The red stove, old as I am, must be
polished at all times. You don't know this about me.
I do it when you're not home.

The Magic Chef gleams in his tipped hat.
Oven shoots to 500 when you set it low.
Then fluctuates. Like a personality.

Thanks to my mother I now have an oven thermometer
but must open the oven door to check it.

Even when a cake's in there. Isn't this supposed to be
disaster for a cake?

My mother does crosswords, which I will never do.
But a word spelled wrongly anywhere
prickles my skin. Return to beginning
with pencil, black ink.
Cross you at the "a." Rearrange.
We had family discussions
about a preference for the British *grey.*
In the spelling bee I tripped on *reveille,*
a bugle call, a signal at dawn.
I have risen early
ever since.

*Linda Pastan with her
daughter Rachel.*

Linda Pastan's grandfather.

LINDA PASTAN

I write my poems about what is most important and most present in my life, and what could be more important, more present, than family—parents, grandparents, children? Now that I have grandchildren of my own, seven of them, I have started writing grandchildren poems. Where the roots go deep, we look for new blossoms.

NOTES FROM THE DELIVERY ROOM

Strapped down,
victim in an old comic book,
I have been here before,
this place where pain winces
off the walls
like too bright light.
Bear down a doctor says,
foreman to sweating laborer,
but this work, this forcing
of one life from another
is something that I signed for
at a moment when I would have signed anything.
Babies should grow in fields;
common as beets or turnips
they should be picked and held
root end up, soil spilling
from between their toes—
and how much easier it would be later,
returning them to earth.
Bear up . . . bear down . . . the audience
grows restive, and I'm a new magician
who can't produce the rabbit
from my swollen hat.

She's crowning, someone says,
but there is no one royal here,
just me, quite barefoot,
greeting my barefoot child.

A REAL STORY

Sucking on hard candy
to sweeten the taste
of old age,
grandpa told us stories
about chickens,
city chickens sold
for Sabbath soup
but rescued at the end
by some chicken-loving
providence.

Now at ninety-five,
sucked down
to nothing himself,
he says he feels
a coldness;
perhaps the coldness David felt
even with Abishag
in his bed
to warm
his chicken-thin bones.

But when we say
you'll soon get well,
grandpa pulls the sheet

over his face,
raising it between us
the way he used to raise
the Yiddish paper
when we said
enough chickens
tell us a real story.

Willie Perdomo and his mother, Carmen.

WILLIE PERDOMO

I've never known "family" in the traditional Thanksgiving-get-together sense. I remember the first day I saw the apartment where my mother still resides. We had just returned from an appointment downtown. Although it was only a six-story project, the building looked immense and intimidating. The apartment was empty, and the walls were painted bone-white. My mother opened the door to a room and said, "This is your room, Papo." Her voice bounced back from the room, deep and thunderous. There was a bright red Tonka fire truck on the windowsill. A light breeze helped it roll back and forth and I just stood looking at the truck, clenching my mother's hand, and from then on it was just me and Mami making it in the world.

She's my family. There are no remaining relatives from her side. I attended middle and upper school at a lower-Manhattan prep school, and classmates would ask me what my mother did for a living because their mothers were doctors, lawyers, and executives. Their mothers were on the board of trustees at such-and-such corporation. So as I started to develop a voice, I decided to write a poem for my mother and called it "Unemployed Mami." It's my answer to my classmates. An early divorce denuked whatever I knew of a nuclear family, so I pretty much looked to my friends for family.

In May 2000, I took my first trip to Puerto Rico in twenty years and found my grandfather, Pellín Perdomo, who is eighty-four years old and living with his wife, Lydia, in Ponce. He is a troubadour. I like to think that I have poetry and music running in my blood. I know that my great-grandfathers came from the Canary Islands and Cuba, and finally settled in Puerto Rico. In July, I will be visiting my father and siblings, so roots are starting to make their way into my family tree.

UNEMPLOYED MAMI

Even though she don't have a job mami still works hard.
The last twenty-three years of her life haven been spent
teaching a poet and killing generations of cockroaches
with sky-blue plastic slippers, t.v. guides, and pink tissues.
She prays for the poet as he runs into the street looking
for images of Boricua sweetness to explode in his face.
The young roaches escape in the dark while my unemployed
mami goes to sleep cursing at them.

Even though she don't have a job mami still works hard.
She walked behind my drunken father, in the rain, as he
stumbled into manhood and oblivion in America wearing
his phony mambo king pinky ring. He beat my mami,
he beat my mami, stop beating my mami! with the black
umbrella; the one with the fake ivory horsehead handle.
I still hear the same salsa blaring out the same social club
where I use to fall asleep and dream happy lives.

Even though she don't have a job mami still works hard.
Every year she prays for my abuela who died in a sweet
bed of Holy Water y Ben Gay while the poet was kicking
his mother inside her stomach. Mami looks at Miss America,
Miss Universe, Miss Everything, every year and then she runs
into her bedroom to dig out her high school yearbook from
underneath her pile of "important papers." "Look, Papo.

Look at your mother when she was eighteen years old. She
was pretty like those girls on t.v." You still are, I say.

Even though she don't have a job mami still works hard.
Lately, she plays slow songs of lost love over and over and
over. She looks out the window only when it rains, measuring
tear drops against the rain drops. Where is that man, I wonder,
as I sit in my room writing and rewriting a poem for her.
I catch her peeking at me from the corner of her eye, wondering if
I do, I really do, love you and that's not the record, that's me, I say,
hugging her with a kiss.

Don't cry, mami.
Even though you don't have a job
I know you still be working hard.

Katha Pollitt and Sophie Pollitt-Cohen.

KATHA
POLLITT

I've always felt that motherhood should make a woman more powerful—stronger, more valued, more directly connected to the center of life and society—but in real life it often makes her less so. Women with babies and small children are pushed to the margins in many ways, large and small: When I was pregnant I noticed for the first time the sign in my local post office banning baby carriages and strollers. How did they imagine mothers would buy stamps and pick up their packages? Being pregnant, I found that having a baby was in some ways a very democratic experience for me—suddenly I could have interesting, immediately intimate conversations with just about anybody—the man at the used-book store, the dry cleaner, total strangers. At the same time, I felt that I had been placed in a box—a pretty box, but a box all the same.

"Playground" is about women in that box. The way out would be for mothers to seriously talk to each other—about their marriages and men, their ways of being with their children, their real feelings, their hopes and desires and fears. But it was not possible to have these conversations, because they were too threatening and violated too many taboos and conventions. I've been told I went to the wrong playground. I hope that's true.

PLAYGROUND

In the hygienic sand
of the new municipal sandbox,
toddlers with names from the soaps,
Brandon and Samantha,
fill and empty, fill and empty
their bright plastic buckets
alongside children with names
from obscure books of the Bible.
We are all mothers here,
friendly and polite.
We are teaching our children to share.

A man could slice his way
through us like a pirate!
And why not? Didn't we open
our bodies recklessly
to any star, say, Little one,
whoever you are, come in?
But the men are busy elsewhere.
Broad-hipped in fashionable sweatpants,
we discuss the day—a tabloid
murder, does cold cream work,
those students in China—

and as we talk
not one of us isn't thinking,
Mama! Was it like this?
Did I do this to you?
But Mama is too busy,
she is dead, or in Florida,
or taking up new interests,
and the children want apple juice
and Cheerios, diapers and naps.
We have no one to ask but each other.
But we do not ask each other.

Liz Rosenberg with her son,
Eli, ten months old.

Liz Rosenberg, age seven, and her mother, Lucille.

LIZ
ROSENBERG

I think and write a lot about family; I am not sure I always pay enough attention to them when they are actually in the same *room* with me. This would be a terrible mistake. Poetry is all about connections, from rhymes to metaphors to the simplest idea that we can understand each other's words. Family is the first connection we feel. It lasts a lifetime . . . many lifetimes.

At the root of our first beginnings, and in the flower of our final journey, we are all related. In work and in life, I try to remember this.

WHITE SLIP

Ma, I saw you wearing your satin slip
and a slash of bright lipstick, in my dream.
We must have been going to a party,
the closet stood wide open.
I waited in a plain white cotton slip,
one small flower embroidered on the chest
while you leaned to the mirror, putting on your face.

Expectant hours:
the decorated party plates
emptied and cleaned. Nobody wears slips anymore
and my favorite golden-green dress with the yellow daisies
drowned in the last basement flood.

Oh, where is your sequined dress now?
Your beautiful, slippery-scaled orange dress
that hung just out of reach?

HOW QUICKLY, HOW EARLY

The fourth-grader, his puffy down jacket
bloodred as any cardinal,
flies lightly up the path to school, skidding
when he gets to the open door.
Then, looking strangely
like his father heading in to work,
he stops; shoves back his hood,
braces his shoulders
for the day, and trudges forward.
How quickly, how early such
lessons begin!

Molly Bendall, Vivienne St. John, and David St. John, 1999.

DAVID
ST. JOHN

Poetry is the language of intimacy, the language with which we speak of the things that matter most to us. And so, poetry is also the language of the family. Poetry allows us to share what otherwise might remain hidden. We all know that our deepest fears, hopes, and desires often resist being spoken of in the light of day. Poetry helps us to say what otherwise might seem to us unsayable. The members of a family who share poetry are also sharing the most intimate aspects of themselves. Poetry *is* family.

HUSH
For My Son

The way a tired Chippewa woman
Who's lost a child gathers up black feathers,
Black quills & leaves
That she wraps & swaddles in a little bale, a shag
Cocoon she carries with her & speaks to always
As if it were the child,
Until she knows the soul has grown fat & clever,
That the child can find its own way at last;
Well, I go everywhere
Picking the dust out of the dust, scraping the breezes
Up off the floor, & gather them into a doll
Of you, to touch at the nape of the neck, to slip
Under my shirt like a rag—the way
Another man's wallet rides above his heart. As you
Cry out, as if calling to a father you conjure
In the paling light, the voice rises, instead, in me.
Nothing stops it, the crying. Not the clove of moon,
Not the woman raking my back with her words. Our letters
Close. Sometimes, you ask
About the world; sometimes, I answer back. Nights
Return you to me for a while, as sleep returns sleep
To a landscape ravaged
& familiar. The dark watermark of your absence, a hush.

Kate Schmitt with her younger sister, Kristie.

KATE
SCHMITT

The way I came to poetry was through family—my parents read to me as a child, for instance—but also because we are poems ourselves—the poems of our parents. I remember the hour I spent in my grandfather's basement in upstate New York reading my grandmother's poems, a woman who died long before I was born. The basement wasn't well lit, and it was damp. I was leaning on an old Ping-Pong table and trying to absorb all that I could under the bare lightbulb. I was amazed at how the poems were still the same even though she was gone, and amazed because she was writing about the same things that I was. (There was even a poem that had a line nearly identical to one of mine.) So that ability to communicate across time and distance seems important to poetry; a way of speaking without the boundaries that our lives have.

LEAVING YOU

for Kristie

Just before I left we sat at the kitchen counter
and there was something very sweet
about your child's foot
on top of mine,
the way your arch curled around my anklebone
and cradled it there. I wondered
what you were thinking about, smiling
as if the best thing in the world were right then,
our breakfast and the sun.

I was remembering when you were born.
I would hold you,
your eyes looking at me,
your hand touching my cheek,
my hair, and when sleep
took you, you lay in perfect faith
that I would hold you forever.

Henry M. Seiden (right) with his son and granddaughter.

HENRY M. SEIDEN

One of the pleasures in being a parent is the chance for "do-overs," the opportunity to have some experiences again and to improve on them. For example, you get to create or help to create, and then witness through the eyes of your child, certain kinds of ordinary *magic:* like, say, blowing soap bubbles or building a snowman. Or you get to explain things—so you have to think about things you haven't thought about in a long time. Once, one summer evening when our son Josh was only two and we were outside our rented cottage, I told him, "Look—all those lights in the sky—those are stars!" He looked a moment. "Are they flying, Dad?" he asked me.

MONTY
The Bronx, 1948

Monty always shook my hand and kissed my little sister.
He had a black Buick Roadmaster, the grill of which grinned
like a mouth with chrome teeth.
He had a straw hat in summer and hand-painted ties;
a sweet, insurance agent's drawl, a pack of Luckies
in one shirt pocket and a heavy hearing aid in the other.
He had an ex-wife in Alabama.
He had Montague E. Foote on his ID bracelet,
and a little *m,* big *F,* little *e* on his tiepin, and his cufflinks.
He took my schoolteacher Grandma places: City Island and Atlantic
    City.
He knew fish houses downtown & how to eat a lobster.
He knew what to say—that the best thing to come out of the South
was the train going North.
But after they married, she complained to my mother:
he drank too much and his cough was waking her;
and his teeth came out at night and sometimes
he didn't come in until the next day. He took to sleeping
on the living room rug—for his back, he explained it;
and ate bananas & drank prune juice, finding harmony, I guess,
where he could get it.
He would sit in the window at the kitchen table, in the silence she left
when she left in the morning, in his undershirt,
with his Luckies and coffee and the *Daily Mirror.*

If I walked by that way on my way to school,
he might toss me a banana—to see if I could catch it.
And he bought me a bicycle. And a fishing pole.
And took me fishing once, now I remember it:
his hands shaking too much to bait the hook.

TURTLE STORY

Once we sent Josh home
from the Burns Street park—for a strawberry.
We gave him the key, he was that kind of kid,
he was four and ran all the way and then back
with a berry as big as his fist—for the snapping turtle
which Bobby Hussian had just come back with
from visiting his father in the country. Bobby'd said:
It eats *strawberries.* We doubted that. We gathered
in a circle, parents & children in the fading summer light
—I think the light was fading but that may be the romantic
in me. Did I say it was a Sunday afternoon in June?
The turtle was refusing to come out, an imitation of a coffin
the size of a grown man's hand. Can you see
the scene? the park, the light, the circle of parents
and children, the turtle on the grass, the strawberry placed
in front of it, the red, the green. The turtle stirs a little,
extends its head. This is the first we've seen it *has* a head.
It takes a turtle-step toward the strawberry, graceful
in a way, smoother than you might think from anything
you think you know of turtles. It takes a bite! Another bite!
It is voracious. Can you say that about turtles?
It was a kind of miracle. The turtle ate the strawberry!
Have you ever heard a story where everyone
lived happily ever after—and you believed it?
It was something like that.

Jason Shinder (center) with his brother and sister.

JASON
SHINDER

My father and I were attending a memorial service at a nearby temple for a friend of the family, Rabbi Stein. I was in my second year of college, had been doing some writing, and, on this occasion, wrote a brief eulogy. I had known Rabbi Stein well. Between my tenth and thirteenth years we often walked together, just the two of us, in a lively air of conversation, to and from Temple.

After I delivered the eulogy, my father leaned over to me and whispered abruptly, "That's what I would have said, if I could have written it."

That was all he said. I suspected, however, in his words a meaning that had never been so clear to me before. He seemed to be saying: Each in our own time and nature might contribute something to life's vision and direction.

This idea has revealed itself again and again, with more and more clarity, as I've experienced the love between the members of my family, as well as our occasional anger and shortsightedness. All of us are linked in our efforts to contribute, to be decent, and to speak to each other and the world outside.

I feel blessed to have fallen in love at an early age with what can be such a beautiful and honest communicator as poetry. It often feels the rhythms of the poems I first fell in love with then, by poets such as Housman, Auden, or Thomas (as well as the rhythms of the poems I fall in love with today) still hold me when I'm silent or trying to say or do whatever is the next joyful or difficult necessary thing.

PLACES HE WASN'T

Just once more I want to hear
the way my father said EHHH
in one breath, his mouth barely opening
after hearing one more story
of how the future was so close,
so far away. It was the slow downward whining
by which his life was given meaning.
Some misery rose in his veins
and the vowels and consonants locked
at the back of his throat.

EHHH. The longing to be places he wasn't.
After the mortgage wolfed down the faces
of the weekly one hundred dollar bills,
after the wheels of his new Lincoln Continental
turned over the same gravelly roads.
Just once more I want to sit beside
him before the turkey and potatoes
and hear his earthly prayer, his poem.

BECAUSE ONE IS ALWAYS LEAVING

Especially
     in the late afternoon,
          when my nieces

close their eyes
     and bend
          their heads

to inhale
     the bubbles that rise
          from the tall glasses

of milk,
     licking the white juice
          off their lips

that open
     on the softened-stained
          black and white cookies

that have been
     dipped
          into the glass

and then dipped
     again,
          sopping with cream,

I like to think
        about stopping
                the passage of time—

not a bird,
        not a branch
                in bloom,

not an insect
        stirring
                in the still grasses and ferns.

Gary Soto.

*Gary Soto with his wife, Carolyn,
and his daughter, Mariko.*

GARY
SOTO

Since my family wouldn't go away, I took advantage of their presence and wrote about them. Over the years I have peopled my poems and essays with my brothers and sister, mother and deceased father, my stepfather, neighbors who were like family, family who were like neighbors. I also included the family animals—Blackie our dog, Boots our cat, the canaries, and poor Brownie the inferior dog who could do nothing but cough and limp. After twenty-seven years of writing, I look at my work; if family had never been a part of my life, then a good portion of my work would never have been written. I would have less to say about my years.

WORRY AT THE END OF THE MONTH

The perfect life overturns like a red wagon.
My wife is doing her nails.
Her breasts are heavy, she is late,
And I'm pacing up and down like a mad doctor.

Now I see it all:
A baby fat as a water bottle
Swaddled in a blue blanket.
Is he smiling for Grandma's Kodak?
Is he burping the milk of pleasure?
Is he kicking his feet for song?
No, he's grunting with one hand on my nose.

Adios to my Italian clothes,
My rack of wines, my dear friends,
My car glinting evilness on all four bumpers,
The crown of cleverness on my head deflating like a cake.

Adios to my weekend trips,
Pacific Grove, behind the finely ground lenses
Of German binoculars, the sea as blue as a made-up heaven;
Where whales sing, tourists look,
And the three-flavored ice-cream cones totter
In our hands
As we go from shop to shop.

The good life ends.
Evenings I will stay home
And watch the fireplace with its saw of red flames,
My daughter reading, my wife reading,
My pit bull Apollo cleaning his paw,
With Dinner Jazz on the radio,
Piano noise like the footsteps of a divorced man

Walking up stairs. I will stare
At my bankbook, worry my brow into lines,
And rinse my throwaway shaver over and over.

Now what will my daughter say?
Cry? Lecture me on self-control?
Conspire with Apollo, heathen dog
Who, I know in my heart, has always eyed
My legs as a second helping of Mexican food?

I'm too old to start over. The hair
On my pillow could smother a kingly rat.
My brow is lined, my bones a wobbly chair.
Give a week, a month, he'll be here,
Bundle that's my life, child for the next century,
Hoodlum out for my sleep, my son, my son,
Bald, pink, with fists beating sparks from my sleepy eyes.

Bettye T. Spinner and her daughter and granddaughter.

BETTYE T. SPINNER

Poetry involves great risk, for both the writer and the reader. You see, the pen in the poet's hand pierces layers of our world and often reveals truths we never guessed were there, just beneath the surface, waiting to be realized and expressed. When a poem touches us, we feel in it the image of ourselves. We touch the pulse of human connection to siblings, our parents and grandparents, to generations of our forebears whose names we may not know, but whose blood pumps through our veins with every heartbeat. Poems, like ourselves, are rooted in ancestral memory. Both are challenges to us to make our lives flower.

HER STORY

Speak to me of strong slave women,
of a great-grandmother who plowed
in southern fields from first light into dusk,
who hoed and raked the rows of tobacco
and swallowed her labor pains.

Tell how she crouched low in the field
to birth her child, how she dropped him
like seed on loosened earth and willed
that he survive. Repeat, repeat for me
how she bit the cord and tied it,
how she wiped her newborn clean,
then swaddled him in the skirt she
haltered high to hold the tiny seed
close to the warm soil of her breast,
there to suckle when and if he could
through long hours of toil left in her day.

Fill my ears, fill my mind with this litany,
and I will tell you how a martyr's roots
entwine her children, how they embrace
the source from which daughters spring.
I bear witness to her strength alive today
in seven sisters and their female issue,
who reap the harvest of her mother courage,
of grain she sowed in furrows of the heart,
in needful acts no history books record.

Gerald Stern with his daughter, Rachel,
and granddaughter Rebecca.

GERALD
STERN

For some reason I have written several poems about my daughter, as well as the other women in my life—my dead sister, my former wife, my mother—but few, if any, about my son. The issue is therefore, clearly, my relationship with women. My daughter, Rachel, is my firstborn; we were and are very close. As usual in these cases, there are unsolved—and unsolvable—issues. *Nu?* I love her, and her new daughter, Rebecca.

WAVING GOOD-BYE

I wanted to know what it was like before we
had voices and before we had bare fingers and before we
had minds to move us through our actions
and tears to help us over our feelings,
so I drove my daughter through the snow to meet her friend
and filled her car with suitcases and hugged her
as an animal would, pressing my forehead against her,
walking in circles, moaning, touching her cheek,
and turned my head after them as an animal would,
watching helplessly as they drove over the ruts,
her smiling face and her small hand just visible
over the giant pillows and coat hangers
as they made their turn into the empty highway.

Deborah Tall with her daughter Zoe Tall Weiss, November 1984.

DEBORAH
TALL

I began talking to my eldest daughter months before she was born. She already had opinions: She'd kick her disapproval if I switched the tape deck from Bach to Bartók (a musical preference she still firmly holds to). I had opinions, too—worries, joys—but had a harder time conveying them to her, not being inclined to kick back. My side of the conversation found its home in poetry. I recorded her story, from conception to birth, a monologue I figured she'd someday read and have the chance to respond to. Now, at fifteen, she's mostly embarrassed by those poems. Of "Touched" she'd say it just proves how overprotective I am! But I still wish her and her sister to be touched only by love.

TOUCHED

At the ballet,
a woman sits down beside me,
sticks her hands on my pregnant belly, says,
"How are *we* tonight?"

Her embarrassed teenage daughter sinks
into the next seat
while you let loose
with a few good thumps.

I don't know why I tell you this—
you seemed to enjoy at least the music
and you'll soon meet many faces like that woman's
coming at you uninvited.

But I want you to know
how sad it made me—
this first time you were touched by someone
who wasn't going to love you.

Philip Terman and his daughter Miriam.

PHILIP
TERMAN

As they are for many poets, ancestry and family are important sources for my work. Poetry tries to explore the mystery of relationships and the poet's connections with past and future. I think my Jewishness, its emphasis on the family, the past, and its commitment toward the future has influenced me to explore those areas. My ancestors were instrumental in determining who I am; writing poems about them (or about imagining them) lets me both communicate with them and preserve their lives through writing about them.

It's strange that I should be writing so many poems about my father, who died ten years ago, because we didn't speak very much while he was alive. Writing about him now might be his way of communicating through me, our way of speaking to each other on a deeper level. Now I find myself writing poems about my daughter, poetry deepening my understanding of the nature of time and continuum, how the spirit of life evolves and renews itself.

INSTRUCTIONS ON CLIMBING YOUR FATHER'S GARAGE

At first sign of dark,
climb onto the window ledge—
flatten your hands
on the roof's peeled tar:
all of your body is muscle,
sweat and strain, until
you rise against this
downward stress. Stand
full-length and walk
on the strange surface
twelve feet up. Look down
through the basketball net
to the other side. See,
just a few feet beyond,
your father has switched on
the kitchen light: he paces
in and out of your vision,
looking for something, for you.
Turn to the far corner, face
the neighbor's back yard,
sit down, legs dangling
over the edge. Looking into
the millions of stars, count,
until he calls, your blessings.

Antonio Vallone and his son, Johnny.

ANTONIO VALLONE

Last fall, my five-year-old son, John Anthony Atkins Vallone, wrote his first poem. Johnny, as everyone calls him, is named for three great-grandfathers, a grandfather, a great-uncle, an uncle, and me. My wife and I have also given him her family name, which she continues to use. My wife's family has several artists, and mine had a hat designer with some panache, but mostly we come from immigrant, blue-collar backgrounds. I'm the first poet, though perhaps not the last.

This is Johnny's poem:

Winter Dragons

Fall is the time when trees turn into rainbows
The clouds look like polar bears
The hanging icicles look like dragons' teeth.

My wife and I love the poem because it's truly his. That is, his personality, or what the poet Li-Young Lee calls "presence" radiates from the words for us. Long after Johnny's grown into the man we believe he will become, long after his winter dragons have melted into the caverns of memory, the poem will bring us back to the boy he is now.

Family is one way we help keep alive whatever's precious to us—our DNA, beliefs, rituals, history, stories, memories. Poetry is another.

Poetry is as important as family and as often ignored until it's really needed. Every child could save the world. Even the darkest poem has a glimmer of hope because someone is telling it. Like raising a child, you do your best with a poem for as long as it lets you, and then you send it out alone, hoping it will be able to fend for itself, make its way without harm, find someone to fall in love with it and bring it home.

PEACH BLOSSOM SNOW

I forget where I am.
Standing under a telephone pole, I watch wind-blown snowflakes
appear out of the distant blue twilight
and flutter through a streetlight's yellow glow
into my hands, and I am a boy
standing under my grandfather's two-story peach tree
in late afternoon sunshine, scooping up cool handfuls
of peach blossoms from heaps I made
with my feet, trying to toss them
back into branches
I can't reach.
It was June or July.
I was in my grandfather's backyard garden at 45 Martin Street
in Rochester, New York. Snowflakes fell, and still fall,
over my head. Or were they, are they,
peach blossoms I couldn't, and still can't, catch
on my tongue . . . ?
What am I doing?
The tree's black branches break
clear from memory into my mind,
and the scent of peach blossoms holds me
like my grandfather's voice calling my name to bring me
back home at dusk. My grandfather and his peach tree live
in the light,
in their own light

and the light within. Now,
as a gust of wind brushes against my cheek, I look down.
I step off the curb onto a street
in West Lafayette, Indiana. It is February.
The snowflakes in my hands have melted,
and still melt, instantly into the hands
of the past, into the patient tongue
of memory. The ghosts
of snowflakes fade darkly
into my shoes like stains from crushed peach blossoms. . . .
Where am I now?
The scattered peach blossoms gather
on the road. Shuffling the long way
toward home,
I plow them into piles
with my feet, toss them
back into the wind and twilight,
and I watch as they flutter down
around me
into my grandfather's garden.

FROM LEARNING TO DANCE

I insisted on drawing the drapes before my mother
box-stepped with me in the living room, both of us
counting out loud: "one, two, three, and
one, two, three, and,"

flattening out the shag rug's nap
and kicking dust into the secret twilight.
The whole time I stared down
at my feet, going in their own directions.

I was all follow and never remembered
which arm hooked around the waist
to pull my partners within a phone book's width of me
(the proper Catholic distance) and which arm was crooked up

in that polite, uncomfortable posture
to hold their hands. I was happy
my friends couldn't see me
stepping off the plot of my grave

one square foot after another. More than anything,
I wanted to hang myself
over girls' shoulders in the junior high gym,
slipping my sweaty hands like a thief

into the back pockets of their jeans.
I wanted to fling myself around
in primitive ways like the white tribe
I studied Saturdays on *American Bandstand.*

But these were Sunday afternoons in the suburbs
of Rochester, New York. Mario Lanza sang
Italy's greatest hits
from the Victrola's speakers, the volume turned low

for the neighbors. All my mother had to show
for her trouble for giving in to my pleading
was sore feet and stubbed toes.
Nights, she soaked my clumsy mistakes

out of them in a pan of hot water and Epsom salts.
But every Sunday she was ready again.
When "Arrivederci Roma" or one of our other favorites played,
I felt thankful she was holding me safe.

I thought ahead to the terrifying mysteries
I hoped were waiting:
tango, rumba, waltz, fox-trot,
Krista Adams, Shari Coopersmith, Nancy Lysko, Bonnie Chasteen.

CAMPING OUT IN THE BACKYARD

To hold off sleep, my cousin Mike and I swore
and punched each other on the arms.

Twilight crept out from under roots and rocks,
hoarding shadows and sneaking up on us.

The twelve pines my uncle planted lined up
like mute angels.
                        The willow became a man,
black suit and overcoat blowing in the wind.

The powdery odor of lilacs was perfume
worn by old women at funerals.

I squinted through my glasses into the dark.
Even my cousin's better eyes went blind.

Like a black skeleton, the clothes pole reached
out, rapped me on the head with its bony arm.

I stumbled, and an owl called *who, who, who,*
the sound of breath over an open grave.

We talked about stars that looked like bullet holes,
the bloody moon hidden by shreds of clouds.

Something scraped against the tent. Leaves scampered
across the opening like thin, brown rats.

Flashlights in front of us like swords, we hacked
a path into the house to save our mothers.

Li-Shen Yun and her grandmother.

LI-SHEN YUN

When I was five years old, I went out to a hill in Vermont with my grandmother. I coaxed her into getting on a saucer-sled and then pushed her down the hill! Well, she survived the wild ride and scolded me. What amazed me was how spirited my grandma was.

Grandmother came from a farming village in Toisan, China, where it never snowed. The first time she ever rode on a plane was on her journey to America. Today, at ninety-four years old, she has a lot of spirit, and has lived through most of the twentieth century and into the twenty-first. She survived famine, war, loss, and revolution. Now she has ten great-grandchildren. She believes in everyone doing their part—when she dries her hands, she takes only one paper towel, because she says, everyone has to share. She is strong physically and mentally—she does tai chi every morning and goes to the Buddhist temple. When I visit, she likes to make me special herbal soups. I am still learning new things about my grandma. On a recent visit, I discovered she likes to watch football on TV! Grandma became an American citizen last year.

SATURDAY IN CHINATOWN

Every Saturday I visit my grandmother.
Like thousands of the faithful
after college, employed
"erudite"

guilty
frustrated
by the silence

no speaky

Chinese

no speaky

English.

I climb
steep stairs
of a narrow
building
beige paint
peeling
ceiling
slung low
steps kneeling
to the next

American made
grandchild.

I smile
as she peers up carefully
from the crack
in the door.

Every Saturday I visit my grandmother.
She makes me soup.
I slurp carelessly
while she sits
alone
dark
on a small wooden stool.
Quiet
eyes blinking
hands folded
feet unbound.

She had a man once
across the ocean
but now her worn face is
silent
far away.

"Grandma" I say softly.
She stares into space.
I let her be.

BIOGRAPHICAL NOTES

MARVIN BELL grew up in the small town of Center Moriches on eastern Long Island, where he now spends part of each year. He also lives in Iowa City, Iowa— where he teaches, and has recently been named Iowa's State Poet Laureate—and Port Townsend, Washington. He is the author of seventeen books of poetry and essays. His newest book of poems is *Nightworks: Poems 1962–2000,* from Copper Canyon Press.

His father and mother's names are Saul and Belle; his wife is Dorothy Ann (maiden name: Murphy), his sons are Nathan Saul and Jason Aaron; his daughter-in-law is Leslie Irene (maiden name: Chapman); and his grandchildren are Colman Saul and Aileen Violet.

ROBERT BLY is a poet, storyteller, mentor of young poets, antiwar activist, translator, essayist, philosopher, editor, and lecturer. Some of his books are *Morning Poems; What Have I Ever Lost by Dying?; The Morning Glory; A Little Book on the Human Shadow; Iron John: A Book about Men;* and *The Sibling Society,* among others. Several of his works and lectures are available on audiotape, including *The Divine Child,* with Marion Woodman, and *Into the Deep.* He and his wife, Ruth, live together near a lake in Minnesota.

DAVID BOSNICK has worked for the past fifteen years as owner of independent bookstores and director of college bookstores. He has published stories and poems in *MSS, Tar River Poetry, The Carolina Quarterly,* and elsewhere. He says of himself, "David Bosnick lives in a dream."

MICHAEL BURKARD was born and raised in Rome, New York. Among his many books of poems are *My Secret Boat* (W. W. Norton, 1990) and *Entire Dilemma* (Sarabande Books, 1998). He has two more books of poems forthcoming in 2001: *Unsleeping* (Sarabande Books) and *Pennsylvania Collection Agency* (New

Issues Press). Michael teaches in the M.F.A. program at Syracuse University and also at the Fine Arts Work Center in Provincetown, Massachusetts.

DAVID CHIN grew up in Jersey City, New Jersey, and attended public schools, Antioch College, Columbia, and the State University of New York at Binghamton. He studied ophthalmology and biology and made his living for a time as a biological engineer. His poems have appeared in *Chalked in Orange* (Mbirra Press) and in *The China Cupboard and the Coal Furnace* (Mellen Poetry Press.) He lives in Dallas, Pennsylvania, with his wife, Lorna, and his daughter, Rachel. He teaches at Penn State University's Wilkes-Barre campus.

VICTORIA CLAUSI earned her M.F.A. degree in poetry from Bennington College, where she now teaches poetry in the July Program. She also works as a staff alumni liaison for Bennington's writing programs office. Her limited-edition chapbook *Boarding House* (1999) was published through Bennington College's M.F.A. in Writing Alumni Chapbook Series. Ms. Clausi's poems have also appeared in *Poetry Motel, Visions International,* and *Squaw Valley Review.*

STEPHEN DOBYNS has published ten books of poems, twenty novels, essays on poetry (*Best Words, Best Order,* St. Martin's Press, 1996), and a collection of short stories (*Eating Naked,* Holt/Metropolitan 2000). His most recent book of poems is *Pallbearers Envying the One Who Rides* (Penguin 1999). Two of his novels, *Cold Dog Soup* and *The Two Deaths of Señora Puccini* have been made into films. He has taught at universities and colleges, including the University of New Hampshire, Boston University, the University of Iowa, and in the M.F.A. program at Warren Wilson. He was a general-assignment reporter for the *Detroit News* and is presently a guest writer for the *San Diego Reader.* Mr. Dobyns lives with his family near Boston.

MARIA MAZZIOTTI GILLAN is the author of seven books of poetry, including *Where I Come From: New and Selected Poems* (Guernica) and *Things My Mother Told Me* (Guernica). She is the founder and director of the Poetry Center at Passaic County Community College, and the editor of *The Paterson Literary Review.* Along with her daughter, Jennifer Gillan, she edited *Unsettling America: An Anthology of Contemporary Multicultural Poetry* (Viking Penguin), *Identity Lessons* (Penguin Putnam), and *Growing Up Ethnic in America* (Penguin Putnam).

EAMON GRENNAN is from Dublin and lives and teaches in Poughkeepsie, New York, where he is the Dexter M. Ferry Jr. Professor of English at Vassar College. *Relations: New and Selected Poems* appeared from Graywolf Press in 1998. His volume of translations *Leopardi: Selected Poems* (Princeton University Press) received the 1997 PEN Award for Poetry in Translation. A collection of essays, *Facing the Music: Irish Poetry in the Twentieth Century*, was published recently by Creighton University Press. His other works published in Ireland and the United States include *Wildly for Days* (1983), *What Light There Is* (1987), *What Light There Is and Other Poems* (1989), *As If It Matters* (1991), *So It Goes* (1995).

DONALD HALL has been writing poems and prose since early childhood. Influenced by summer visits to the family farm in rural New Hampshire, he lives today on that same land, at Eagle Pond Farm. Donald Hall writes every day and makes his living by writing poems, prose, translations, children's books, plays, and essays on everything from American poetry to baseball. Some of his best-known books are *The Old Life, Without,* and *The Ox-Cart Man.* His work is also available on audiocassette and in a number of documentaries on video, including *A Life Together,* with his late wife, the poet Jane Kenyon, which aired on PBS as part of *Bill Moyers' Journal.* It is available from Films for the Humanities and Sciences (800-257-5126).

MARIE HOWE was born in Rochester, New York, and received an M.F.A. from Columbia University in 1983. Her first book of poems, *The Good Thief,* was selected by Margaret Atwood for the 1987 National Poetry Series and was published by Persea Books in 1989. She also edited, with Michael Klein, *In the Company of My Solitude: American Writing from the AIDS Pandemic,* published by Persea Books in 1995. She worked for a time as a high-school teacher and now teaches in the writing programs of Sarah Lawrence College, Columbia University, and NYU. Her most recent book is *What the Living Do* (W. W. Norton).

ADRIENNE E. IANNIELLO was born and raised in the Hudson Valley region of New York State. In 2000 she received her B.A. in Italian literature and creative writing from the State University of New York at Binghamton. "Memory" is Adrienne's first published work.

MILTON KESSLER taught for thirty-five years at the State University of New York at Binghamton in the creative writing program, which he founded and shaped.

Among his books of poems are *A Road Came Once, Sailing Too Far,* and *The Grand Concourse* (MSS Press). He also lived and taught abroad in Japan and Israel. A high-school dropout, he called his life in art and teaching "a miracle" and described himself as a singer and poet. In fact, he sang at the Metropolitan Opera in New York City as a young man and later worked in that city's Garment District before earning his degree at the University of Washington. Milton Kessler died unexpectedly in the spring of 2000—after recovering from a quintuple bypass operation—a few weeks before his seventieth birthday. He is survived by his wife, Sonia, his sons David and Daniel, and his daughter, Paula, as well as three grandsons.

MAXINE KUMIN is a Pulitzer Prize–winning poet, writer, children's book author, horse trainer, and essayist. Her newest book, *Inside the Halo and Beyond* (W. W. Norton), tells the story of a terrible accident and its aftermath, which reviewer Carolyn Heilbrun describes as "an earthly miracle wrought by family devotion, gardens, horses, guts."

STANLEY KUNITZ welcomed his ninety-fifth year in 2000 by being named Poet Laureate of the United States and publishing *The Collected Poems* (Norton). In 1995, his collection *Passing Through* (Norton) won the National Book Award. He has received nearly every honor bestowed upon a poet in this country, including the Pulitzer and Bollingen Prizes, a National Medal of the Arts from President Clinton in 1993, and the Frost Medal for lifetime achievement from the Poetry Society of America in 1995. He has served as Consultant in Poetry to the Library of Congress (now called U.S. Poet Laureate), State Poet of New York, and Chancellor of the Academy of American Poets. As editor of the Yale Younger Poets Series from 1969 to 1977 and as a founder of both the Fine Arts Work Center in Provincetown, Massachusetts, and Poets House in New York City, he has promoted poetry and public access to the arts, encouraging many of the younger poets and artists who are now prominent figures in American culture. Kunitz and his wife, the painter Elise Asher, live in New York City and in Provincetown, where the poet maintains a celebrated seaside garden.

GREG KUZMA is the author of *What Poetry Is All About,* a book about poetry. His *Selected Poems* will be published by Carnegie Mellon University Press. Backwaters Press will publish *All That Is Not Given Is Lost,* a first book of longer poems. Greg is presently teaching himself the art of screenwriting.

Rich Landers was born in Hoisington, Kansas, in 1969. When he was two years old, his family moved to Brazil, where he grew up in the cities of Belem and Rio de Janeiro. He was educated at King's College and Yale Divinity School. At Yale he studied poetry with Wayne Koestenbaum and has attended writing conferences at Colgate University and Hartwick College. In July 1999 Rich taught a writing workshop to young people during the week of arts camp at Pathfinder Lodge in Cooperstown, New York. He lived in New York State for nine years, including four years in South New Berlin where he was pastor of the First Baptist Church. Rich is a minister in the American Baptist Churches and currently serves at the Hyde Park Union Church in Chicago, Illinois.

Shara McCallum was born in Jamaica and immigrated at the age of nine to the United States with her family. Her first book of poems, *The Water Between Us,* won the Agnes Starrett Prize and was published by the University of Pittsburgh Press in 1999. She has taught poetry writing and literature to elementary-school children, college students, and adults.

Margaret K. Menges lives in Elmira, New York, the town where she grew up in a family with two younger brothers and an older sister. She teaches middle-school students and has two sons, David and Daniel.

Jerry Mirskin grew up in New York City and Long Island. He has worked on a dairy farm in New York and as a carpenter in New York, California, Maine, and Wisconsin. In addition, he has worked as a New York State Poet-in-the-Schools. In 1993 Camellia Press published a chapbook of Jerry's poems. Jerry's full-length book of poems, *Picture a Gate Hanging Open and Let That Gate Be the Sun,* was chosen as the winner of the Mammoth Press Prize in Poetry and will be published in 2000. Jerry is currently an associate professor at Ithaca College. He has a son, Noah, who is eight years old. Jerry is married to Wendy Dann, a theatrical director. Jerry, Wendy, and Noah live in Ithaca, New York.

Greg Moglia teaches high-school science as well as education and philosophy courses at New York University. He lives in Huntington, New York, near a beautiful duck pond.

Kyoko Mori was born in Kobe, Japan, and moved to the American Midwest in 1977. She is the author of a book of poems, *Fallout;* two coming-of-age novels,

Shizuko's Daughter and *One Bird;* and two nonfiction books, *The Dream of Water: A Memoir* and *Polite Lies: On Being Caught Between Two Cultures.* Her novel *Stone Field, True Arrow* was published in 2000. She is currently a Briggs-Copeland Lecturer in Creative Writing at Harvard University.

MEGEEN MULHOLLAND is the youngest of eight children. She has four brothers and three sisters, all of whom have informed her work in valuable ways. Her mother's contribution has been the greatest of all. Megeen is currently pursuing her doctoral studies in English at the State University of New York at Albany. Her poetry has appeared in *MSS, The Seattle Review, Earth's Daughters, Barkeater,* and other journals.

HOWARD NELSON was born in 1947 in New Jersey. His mother was a junior high school English teacher, and his father was an accountant who commuted every day to New York City. For the past thirty years he has lived in the Finger Lakes region of New York State and taught at Cayuga Community College. He writes essays about poets and other writers, and his books of poems include *Creatures, Singing into the Belly, Gorilla Blessing,* and *Bone Music.*

NAOMI SHIHAB NYE's recent books include *Fuel* (poems), *Habibi* (a novel for teens), and *Lullaby Raft* (a picture book). She has edited five prizewinning anthologies of poetry for young readers, including *This Same Sky, The Tree Is Older Than You Are, The Space Between Our Footsteps: Poems and Paintings from the Middle East,* and *What Have You Lost?*

LINDA PASTAN has published ten volumes of poetry, most recently *Carnival Evening: New and Selected Poems 1968–1998* (W. W. Norton), which was a finalist for the National Book Award. She was Poet Laureate of Maryland from 1991 to 1995 and was on the staff of the Bread Loaf Writers' Conference for twenty years.

WILLIE PERDOMO is the author of *Where a Nickel Costs a Dime* (W. W. Norton). He has been featured on several PBS documentaries including *Words in Your Face* and *The United States of Poetry.* His work has been included in several anthologies, among them *Aloud: An Anthology of Writing from the Nuyorican Poets Café* (Holt) and *Boricuas: An Anthology of Puerto Rican Writing* (One World/Ballantine) and *Listen Up! A Spoken Word Anthology* (Ballantine). Perdomo was the recipient of a

New York Foundation for the Arts Fiction Grant. He cowrote an episode for the HBO series *Spicy City.* He has read and lectured at premier venues in the United States and Europe and has appeared on BBC radio and TV as well as recorded on *Flippin' the Script: Rap Meets Poetry* (Mouth Almighty Records/Mercury). He lives in New York City.

KATHA POLLITT is the author of *Antarctic Traveler* (Knopf, 1982), a book of poems which won the National Book Critics Circle Award, and *Reasonable Creatures: Essays on Women and Feminism* (Knopf, 1994). She writes a column, "Subject to Debate," in *The Nation,* as well as reviews, essays, and articles for many other publications. She lives in New York City with her daughter, Sophie, who turns fourteen in 2001, and Paul Mattick.

LIZ ROSENBERG, born and raised in Syosset, New York, has published three books of poems, including *Children of Paradise* (University of Pittsburgh Press) and *These Happy Eyes,* a new volume of prose poems (Mammoth Press, 2001). She's also published more than a dozen children's books and three other Holt poetry anthologies for young readers. She works with writers, from kindergartners to nonagenarians, and has taught creative writing for twenty-two years at the State University of New York, at Binghamton, where she lives with her husband, son, and their two dogs.

DAVID ST. JOHN is the author of essays, interviews, and seven collections of poems, among them *Hush; The Shore; No Heaven; In the Pines: Lost Poems, 1972–1997* (White Pine Press); and, most recently, *Study for the World's Body: New and Selected Poems* (HarperCollins). *The Red Leaves of Night* (HarperCollins, 1999) was nominated for the *Los Angeles Times* Book Prize in Poetry. His many awards include a Guggenheim Fellowship, the Prix de Rome, and three National Endowment for the Arts fellowships in poetry. He is editor-at-large of *The Antioch Review* and teaches at the University of Southern California. He lives in Venice, California, with his wife, the poet Molly Bendall, and their daughter Vivienne.

KATE SCHMITT was raised in New England but spent part of her childhood in Hong Kong. She earned her bachelor's degree from Colgate University and worked in publishing for a time in Boston before moving to Hong Kong to live with her sister and then later teaching for a year in mainland China. She recently received her master's degree from the University of Texas at Houston.

HENRY M. SEIDEN is a psychologist and psychotherapist who practices in Forest Hills, New York. He has lived there with his wife and children (now grown, with children of their own) since earning his doctoral degree in 1969 from the New School for Social Research. He has published poems in *Poetry, The Humanist, Journal of the American Medical Association,* and elsewhere. He also coauthored, with Christopher Lukas, a book called *Silent Grief: Living in the Wake of Suicide* (Jason Aronson Books).

JASON SHINDER has edited several poetry anthologies on the family, including *First Light* and *Divided Light.* He is also series editor for *Best American Movie Writing: Writing About the Movies,* and author of two collections of his own poetry: *Every Room We Ever Slept In* (Sheep Meadow Press, 1994) and *Among Women,* forthcoming in 2001 from Graywolf Press. Mr. Shinder has worked for the past twenty years for the National YMCA and is currently director of its programs in the arts. He also teaches in the M.F.A. program at Bennington College and at the New School for Social Research.

GARY SOTO's many books include *Living up the Street; Buried Onions; Chato's Kitchen; Nickel and Dime.* In 1999 he won the Literature Award from the Hispanic Heritage Foundation. That same year he accepted the position of Distinguished Professor of Creative Writing at the University of California at Riverside.

BETTYE T. SPINNER has authored two collections of poetry—*Whispers of Generations* and *In the Dark Hush*—and is currently compiling her third, *Faces Behind the Mirror.* A former English teacher, she is now a poetry and diversity consultant, conducting workshops for students and teachers in schools throughout New Jersey, both as freelance and as a Geraldine R. Dodge Foundation poet.

GERALD STERN is the author of eleven books of poetry, including recently *Bread Without Sugar* (W. W. Norton, 1992), *Odd Mercy* (W. W. Norton, 1995), and *This Time: New and Selected Poems* (W. W. Norton, 1998), which won the National Book Award. *Last Blue,* his latest book of poetry, was published in 2000. He has taught at many universities, including Columbia, New York University, Sarah Lawrence, and, until his retirement in 1995, he resided and taught at the Writer's Workshop in Iowa City for fourteen years. He lives now in New Jersey and New York City; he is finishing a new book of poems and writing a kind of memoir.

DEBORAH TALL is a poet, nonfiction writer, teacher, as well as the editor of *Seneca Review*. Her most recent book is *Summons,* winner of the Kathryn Morton Prize for Poetry, published by Sarabande Books. She lives in Ithaca, New York, with her husband, the writer David Weiss, and their two daughters, Zoe and Clea.

PHILIP TERMAN was born in Cleveland, Ohio, and studied at Ohio University, the University of Washington, and Ohio State University. He currently teaches at Clarion University in Pennsylvania. His poetry collection *What Survives* won the Sow's Ear Chapbook Prize in 1993, and his *House of Sages* was published by Mammoth Press in 1998. Philip Terman started the community performance space called the Bridge Coffeehouse and a literary-arts journal *The Oil City Review.* He has taught many kinds of students, including the elderly, the incarcerated, and those returning to school. He lives in a one-room redbrick schoolhouse surrounded by a large garden, with his wife, Chris Hood, and daughter, Miriam.

ANTONIO VALLONE grew up in the city of Rochester, New York, until the age of ten, when he and his family moved to the suburbs. His name, Vallone, means "brave man." He teaches at Penn State University at DuBois, and has published three books of poems, *The Blackbirds' Applause, Grass Saxophones,* and *Golden Carp,* all from the Damballah Press in Chattanooga, Tennessee.

LI-SHEN YUN's poetry can be found in literary journals such as *The Seattle Review, The Georgetown Review,* and *The Paterson Literary Review,* and in anthologies such as *Nuyor-Asian Anthology* (Rutgers University Press) and *Identity Lessons* (Penguin). She has read poems to audiences at many diverse places, from the Langston Hughes Library of New York to the National Library of Singapore.

SUGGESTED READING
AND LISTENING

A Child's Christmas in Wales and Five Poems, Dylan Thomas; audiobook (Harper-Audio). Perhaps the world's most poetic prose, read aloud magnificently by the late Welsh poet Dylan Thomas, *A Child's Christmas in Wales* is a celebration of Christmas, Wales, childhood, and family. Among the five poems recorded here is a great father/son poem, the villanelle "Do Not Go Gentle into That Good Night." (See *Light-Gathering Poems.*)

Divided Light: Father and Son Poems: A 20th Century American Anthology (The Sheep Meadow Press); *Eternal Light: Grandparent Poems: A 20th Century American Selection* (Harcourt); *First Light: Mother and Son Poems: A 20th Century American Selection* (Harcourt); *More Light: Father and Daughter Poems: A 20th Century American Selection* (Harcourt). All four anthologies were edited by poet Jason Shinder. These books were conceived of for "grown-ups" but of course, like most of the books on the list, are equally well suited to astute young readers. All but *Divided Light* are still in print, and readily available.

Earth-Shattering Poems; The Invisible Ladder; and *Light-Gathering Poems* (Henry Holt). All three anthologies were compiled by this editor. *Earth-Shattering Poems* contains poems about life-shattering events—first love, first death, war poems—from Sufi poet Rumi to Pablo Neruda to new voices. *Light-Gathering Poems* was conceived as a companion volume or "antidote" to that collection, with poems of all places and ages that "gather light." *The Invisible Ladder* is a book much like *Roots and Flowers* but about poetry and childhood, with photos of the poets as children and as adults and comments on poetry and childhood.

The Essential Haiku: Versions of Bashō, Buson and Issa, edited by Robert Hass (Ecco Press). If one wishes to learn haiku by great example, this is the book to read. For more explanatory handbooks, try William J. Higginson's fine and thorough *The Haiku Handbook,* or *Seeds from a Birch Tree* by Clark Strand, a spiritual guide to both haiku and life.

Frenchtown Summer, by Robert Cormier (Delacorte Press). From the beloved author of *I Am the Cheese, The Chocolate War,* and other novels, a charming novel in free verse about one boy's coming-of-age in a New England factory town.

Good Woman: Poems and a Memoir, Lucille Clifton (BOA Editions). Alas, this poet was one we were never able to include here. Many of Clifton's poems are about family, poems such as "Conversation with My Grandson, Waiting to Be Conceived," "Forgiving My Father," "The Lost Baby Poem," "My Mama Moved Among the Days." Ms. Clifton is not only a great poet but also a beloved author of many children's books. She won the National Book Award in 2000 for *Blessing the Boats* (BOA Editions).

I, Too, Sing America: Three Centuries of African American Poetry, edited by Catherine Clinton; illustrations by Stephen Alcorn (Houghton Mifflin). A fine, eclectic sampling from three hundred years' worth of African American poetry, with striking artwork.

It's a Woman's World: A Century of Women's Voices in Poetry, edited by Neil Philip. Just as the title suggests, this is a selective and eclectic collection of one hundred years of women's poetry. Contains unforgettable documentary-style photographs.

Knock at a Star: A Child's Introduction to Poetry, revised edition, edited by X. J. Kennedy and Dorothy M. Kennedy (Little, Brown). A new version of a fifteen-year-old classic by the editors of *Talking Like the Rain. Knock at a Star* is the perfect step up from *Talking Like the Rain,* a generously compiled children's version of the *Norton Introduction to Poetry.*

The Norton Introduction to Poetry, seventh edition, edited by J. Paul Hunter (W. W. Norton). This anthology and *The Norton Anthology of Poetry,* as well as *The Norton Anthology of Modern Poetry,* help to make W. W. Norton the premier publisher of English-language poetry in America. *The Norton Introduction to*

Poetry is of the three the least expensive and most accessible to younger poets. It's a comprehensive introductory course in poetry, honed over time and improved upon with each new edition.

Poetry Handbook: A Dictionary of Terms, fourth edition, Babette Deutsch (Harper-Collins). Just what the title suggests, and more—with clear explanations and examples of a wide variety of poetic forms and terms, from *simile* to *villanelle* to *blank verse* to *iambics.*

The Practice of Poetry: Writing Exercises from Poets Who Teach, edited by Robin Behn and Chase Twitchell (HarperCollins). A handbook full of writing exercises, games, and ideas from poets who know and love their craft.

Relatively Speaking: Poems About Family, Ralph J. Fletcher; illustrated by Walter Krudop (Orchard Books). A novel-in-verse told from the viewpoint of an eleven-year-old boy who has a lot to say about his family.

Rose, Where Did You Get That Red? Teaching Great Poetry to Children, Kenneth Koch (Vintage). A contemporary classic, this book remains for many poets and teachers *the* resource on teaching great poetry to children and for helping children to write their own great poetry. Brilliant exercises, as well as examples from famous poets and very young poets, are included.

Strings: A Gathering of Family Poems, edited by Paul Janeczko. This book is out of print, but shouldn't be. It comprises 125 poems on family (none of which appear in this collection). Happily, Janeczko has edited many other highly regarded books still in print, including *Wherever Home Begins: 100 Contemporary Poems* (Orchard Books), which asks the question, What is home? and answers with everything from a roadside cafe to lonely roads to where one's loved ones are. See also Janeczko's own popular poems about baseball in *That Sweet Diamond: Baseball Poems* (Atheneum).

Ten-Second Rainshowers: Poems by Young People, compiled by Sanford Lyme; illustrated by Virginia Halstead (Simon & Schuster). This collection of poems, by some of the thousands of young poets Lyme has taught over a lifetime, is as refreshing as a rain shower and as radiant as the rainbow that follows it.

This Same Sky: A Collection of Poems from Around the World, edited by Naomi Shihab Nye (Simon & Schuster). Naomi Shihab Nye, herself a highly regarded poet, has compiled a number of fine poetry collections for young readers, including *What Have You Lost?* a haunting collection of poems and photos reflecting on loss. *This Same Sky* is a worldwide collection, celebrating the earth with poetry from more than 125 poets from sixty-eight countries.

3 Doz. Poems: From the Writer's Almanac, read by Garrison Keillor; audiotape/CD (High Bridge Company). Poetry lovers of all ages will recognize Garrison Keillor's voice, not only from his popular *Prairie Home Companion* but also from his *Writer's Almanac,* which airs regularly on National Public Radio. Here are thirty-six favorite selections from that series, beautifully read, running the gamut from light verse to Shakespeare, and including many contemporary poets.

Where the Sidewalk Ends, Shel Silverstein; book/audiotape/CD (HarperCollins/HarperAudio/SONY Wonder). I hardly know a young person who doesn't love the work of the late Shel Silverstein, a man who changed the world of children's poetry and gave it new freedom and a sense of play. One can simply buy this book (or any other of his books, such as *A Light in the Attic* and *Falling Up*), but the best way to meet "Uncle Shelby" is to hear him perform his own poems—*read* is too bland a word for what he does. The world misses him.

INDEX OF FIRST LINES

After the oral surgeon, 26
And he said, "Fuck you, fuck you," he
    said. "You're no good," 74
Angela's coming for dinner, he said,
    112
A silver sky, and the lake silver, 101
At first sign of dark, 208
At five I stood amazed watching this
    lion of a man, 125
At "Peking Duck" in Chinatown, 130
At the ballet, 204

Dear Jessie, 36
Driving south in sleet, 73

Especially / in the late afternoon, 188
Even though she don't have a job
    mami still works hard, 159
Every Saturday I visit my
    grandmother, 222

From my father I have inherited the
    ability, 148

Have you even been in a room where
    there are ten pregnant women?,
    141
Here on the table, in an envelope, 18

His first day. Waiting, he plays, 55
How close the clouds press this
    October first, 41

I don't know what you think you're
    doing, 11
I forget where I am, 213
I insisted on drawing the drapes before
    my mother, 215
I'm like those Russian peasant dolls, 50
In the hygienic sand, 164
I told everyone, 45
I wanted to know what it was like
    before, 200
I wish you had knocked on my door
    today, 22

Just before I left we sat at the kitchen
    counter, 176
Just once more I want to hear, 187

Laurel and Hardy wrestle the china
    cupboard, 27

Ma, I saw you wearing your satin slip,
    168
Monty always shook my hand and
    kissed my little sister, 180

My father's back, 78
My grandmother gives me a glass of
    cold water, 119
My mother gave birth to me and I
    never once thanked her, 104
My son, my executioner, 60
My son tells me not to wear my poet's
    clothes, 49

Night and day arrive, and day after
    day goes by, 15

Once on a plane, 145
Once we sent Josh home, 182
Once when night was as black, 108
On the first day of his life, 147

Plump, green-gold, Worcester's pride,
    95
Pop sees me, 118
Praise to my older brother, the
    seventeen-year-old boy, 64

She comes home tired from work, 140
Sitting on a musty recliner, 68

So Dad, my brother said, 124
Speak to me of strong slave women,
    196
Strapped down, 152
Sucking on hard candy, 154

The first in seven years, my uncle
    Shiro's, 132
The fourth-grader, his puffy down
    jacket, 169
The perfect life overturns like a red
    wagon, 192
The way a tired Chippewa woman,
    172
Thought young for the funeral, 136
to a thirteen-year-old sleeping, 10
Today you tell me your mother
    appears, 47
To hold off sleep, my cousin Mike and
    I swore, 217
Tucking you in, blanketing you, 113

Your turn. Grass of confusion, 88
You with the beard as red as
    Barbarossa's, 82